A PIONEER CHRISTMAS BEYOND THE OREGON TRAIL

A WESTERN ADVENTURE NOVELLA

DAVID FITZ-GERALD

CONTENTS

1. Chapter 1   1

2. Chapter 2   11

3. Chapter 3   23

4. Chapter 4   33

5. Chapter 5   44

6. Chapter 6   55

7. Chapter 7   65

8. Chapter 8   74

9. Chapter 9   86

10. Chapter 10   100

Welcome

Merry Christmas from the end of the Oregon Trail in 1850!

This novella is dedicated to all the readers who enjoyed the series, Ghosts Along the Oregon Trail, and were sad to see the family's story come to an end. Instead of letting it end, how about a new beginning instead?

Dorcas and her family have reached their destination, but what happens next? Well, Christmas is coming. It's practically here. These pioneers don't have much, yet they've got spirit. Perhaps that's all they need.

A Pioneer Christmas Beyond the Oregon Trail has been written so that it can also be enjoyed by readers who haven't read the preceding series. It will, of course, be more meaningful for those who complete the journey first. Either way, welcome in. Make yourself at home within these pages.

Thanks for stopping by and joining Dorcas, Agapito, Rose, Andrew, Christopher, and Dahlia Jane as they celebrate their first Christmas in Oregon. And here's to you—may all your Christmases be filled with love, hope, and joy.

CHAPTER 1

Fallen trees surround me. Everywhere I look, there are toppled timbers. Most of them have been brought down by my axe in the five weeks since we reached the end of the Oregon Trail.

How many do we need? It's hard to say. Nobody seems to know. So, I just keep on chopping.

It sounds like awful work but the truth is, I'd do most anything to avoid sewing or hunching over a washboard. Fortunately, my daughter, Rose, is content to do most of those chores.

That tree I've been whacking should be just about ready to fall. Setting the axe down for a moment, I stretch my neck and roll my head.

A loud cracking sound interrupts my brief break. Turning back to look at the tall Douglas Fir, it doesn't take but a moment to realize that it's about to fall.

But something is wrong. It's tilting in the wrong direction.

After making a hasty decision, I tear off toward our encampment, running as fast as my legs will carry me.

My heart thunders in my chest. I know enough to understand that it's impossible to outrun a falling tree. Imagining the wood fibers slowly tearing away near the place where my axe struck the tree, I hope with all my might that it will take longer than usual to crash into the ground.

A creaking sound stretches through the air as I lean forward and try to increase my speed without stepping on the hem of my dress, but I can tell without looking. That tree is coming down fast.

Chopping down trees is dangerous work, but I've been doing it all my life. I've always thought of myself as a lady lumberjack.

Normally, I can tell by instinct what direction a tree will fall. This time, even now, I'm not sure which way it's going. But I know enough to try to get out of the way as fast as I can.

Just when I think I'm in the clear, I feel the slap of branches against my skin. I'm aware of the sting of sharp twigs slicing my shoulders. Then there's a crack at the back of my head.

At first I don't know where I am. I look around and I'm surprised to see my husband and four children looking back at me: Agapito, Rose, Andrew, Christopher, and Dahlia Jane.

I think, *What happened?* And, *Why am I on my back?*

Then the memory comes back in a rush. That Douglas Fir I was chopping down fell in the wrong direction. I tried to outrun it and failed. "How did I get here?" I ask, looking around at my family.

My husband answers, "I carried you, *mi amor*. You screamed, so I came running."

Oh, thank heavens for this man, and the good judgment I showed when I agreed to marry him. "Am I alright, Agapito?"

Agapito looks me over and doesn't seem overly concerned. "It would seem to be so. You have some scratches, bruises, and a growing lump on your head but you should be fine, eventually. Your pretty new dress is not going to make it, Dorcas. You will be needing a new one."

"Good heavens! What a relief."

That wasn't just a pretty new dress. It's the dress I wore for the first time a little more than a month ago when we were married. Good thing I wear men's clothes underneath. Returning to the point, I ask, "How long was I out?"

I always find comfort in his gleaming, antelope eyes. He answers confidently, "It was not long, *mi preciosa*. Maybe three minutes. Not to worry. You will be your regular self in no time."

The truth is, I haven't felt my regular self for the past week or so. Normally, I am unstoppable. I'm used to working from dawn to dark. After six months of marching across the prairies, plains, and deserts of the great American wilderness, and a month of chopping down trees, perhaps I could use a break.

I glance back in the direction of the fallen timbers. It is hard to look upon the devastation. What once was a beautiful stand of lush, green trees now looks like a cyclone has ripped across the land.

As if he can read my mind, Agapito says, "Maybe we have enough timbers now. Seventy five logs for our cabin. A hundred to fence our stock. A few more to build an outhouse. The rest for firewood. Yes, I think maybe we have enough now."

Good heavens. The children. I hope they're not too troubled by what has just happened. I turn my head to see them.

When I look into Rose's eyes, she turns away quickly. "Willow tea. That will help you," she says as she makes her way to the wooden cookstove which is set up under a canvas tarp. She isn't one to say things that don't need saying. The truth is, she's quite a recluse.

Andrew's voice cracks. "Gosh, Mama. That was a close call."

I look at my serious son and think about the newspaper he wrote, documenting every day of our trip from Independence, Missouri to Oregon City. If this had happened while we were emigrating, it would have made the headlines in *The Rolling Home Times*. "Yes. You're right, Andrew. That was way too close."

He hangs his head and says, "I knew something bad was going to happen. I just didn't know what or when. I'm sorry, Mama."

It's the darndest thing. Andrew is always able to predict the weather. Sometimes, he seems to have a strange sense regarding what will happen before it does. He says it's not very reliable. It's kind of silly to think such a thing is possible, but the fact is, he's been correct often enough that we've learned to pay some attention to his preposterous warnings.

Christopher can hardly contain himself. "Heck, Mama. I never seen you run as fast as that. You sure can move when you hafta."

I can't help laughing, but when I do, I realize that my head aches and I feel nauseous. "Whew," I manage to say, "I'm tuckered out but when I'm feeling better, we should have a race, Christopher."

He laughs, slaps his knee, and says, "*You* could never catch *me*, Mama. Maybe you should just give up now. Save yourself the bother!"

Of all my children, that boy reminds me of myself the most. I love them the same, but Christopher and I share a deep love of animals, a wild adventurous spirit, and a passion for the outdoors. "Well, young man, we'll see about that, but just now I could use a little help getting up."

When I'm on my feet, I feel as if my legs might give way. It crosses my mind that I might just crash back to the ground. "Oh dear, you'd better help me find a place to sit for a spell." My vision is blurry and the sun seems way too bright. "Maybe a nice shady spot would do."

Dahlia Jane says, "I've got a perfect spot for you." Her small hand reaches for mine, and Agapito guides me with his arm at my waist. His strong hand is comforting. Dahlia Jane chirps, "Over here, Mama."

When I'm seated, I ask, "Where did this bench come from?"

She answers, "Well, Mama, 'Pito made it for me." She's the only one in the family that calls Agapito, 'Pito for short.

I look at him and his smile confirms it. "It is comfortable, yes?"

Before I can answer him, Dahlia Jane says, "You can use it as long as you want, Mama. I'll sit on the floor."

For a moment, I'm confused. "Oh, on the ground dear. Not the floor. I see." My head throbs and I yawn. "My, oh my. Maybe I should lie down and take a nap."

Agapito says, "Maybe that would not be good. It would be better to stay awake for a while and then we will see."

"Oh, very well." I think to ask for a nice strong cup of coffee but then I recall that Rose is bringing me tea. She's always making that wretched, bitter brew. I'm sure that I'll be fine and consider voicing a protest, but my family will never let me off that easily.

The beginnings of a smile at the corners of Agapito's mouth always turns my heart to mush. I'd best content myself with a break before trying to make myself useful again. With a sigh, I ask him if he could make sure that Rose adds a bit of honey to the foul tea.

The bench is perfectly sized for a small child. It's not a comfortable place for an adult woman, but I refrain from complaining. Why not take a moment to spend some time with my youngest child. The poor thing has spent so much of the past year entertaining herself as we toiled to reach the place of our dreams.

Agapito delivers the tea Rose made and winks at me, knowing how I hate the taste of it. "I will leave you ladies alone but I will check back later."

Andrew and Christopher wear matching frowns as they return to the tasks of stripping bark from logs and splitting rails for fencing. After living in a tent most of the year, they are eager to spend the winter surrounded by solid walls. They never were prone to arguing about having to do the work that living on the frontier requires. We're very lucky.

As the rhythmic taps of Agapito's axe fill our valley, my head swims. I force a few sips of tea down the hatch. After a minute or two, I don't feel as dizzy.

The longer I sit in the dappled sunlight, the more overwhelmed I am by this enchanting setting. The tiny woodland glade looks like a make-believe parlor. It's as if we were indoors. The ground is swept clean, fallen branches and twigs outline the perimeter of a pretend room, and in the center, there's an oddly-shaped stone with a concave, crater-shaped depression on the top.

Dahlia Jane says, "It is for the birds, Mama. Do you like it?"

"Yes, dear. It's very special." A chickadee flits from a tree branch to stand on a rock in the pool of water, dips its beak for a drink, and splashes itself.

Dahlia Jane gestures with her arm as if I weren't already looking at the bird bath. She proudly says, "I keep it full of water. Some birds like to take baths. Others stop by for a drink." My four year old isn't much more talkative than my oldest, but today she chatters happily.

There's a pile of what looks like rocks beside the water. I look closer and ask, "Are those acorns?"

She nods and smiles gleefully. "Yes. When I find nuts I collect them. Birds like to eat them."

I'm surprised when the cream-colored kitten she named Paw climbs out of her pocket. I wonder whether Dahlia Jane's birds will be in danger when

Paw is old enough to be a threat. Thankfully, that kitten stays close to the child. What would we do if it wandered off? It's a terrifying thought.

I hadn't realized that I'd voiced my worry out loud, but Dahlia Jane says, "Christopher told Paw never to hunt birds. Only mice. And he told Paw to stay close by—so we can keep him safe. Paw's a good listener."

Children have such wild imaginations. With a sigh, I look beyond the glade at the towering cone of Mount Hood in the distance. Looking at the dormant volcano always reminds me of the feeling of completing the long journey and all the obstacles we overcame to get here.

After traveling all the way to Oregon, and surviving the disasters that befell so many emigrants, wouldn't it be awful to be done in by a falling tree? As my mind wanders away, Dahlia Jane whispers, "Quiet, Mama. Here comes my friend. She's very shy."

I'm surprised to see a sizeable bird soaring through the air. The feathers under its wings gleam. It's flight is graceful and it lands gently on the rock where the chickadee bathed.

Dahlia Jane whispers, "She's a golden woodpecker."

"Oh." I don't want to say more. If I scare away the bird by talking, it might upset my little girl.

The woodpecker takes a drink. It's quite a sight to behold. I don't think I've ever seen a woodpecker's tongue before. When its thirst is satiated, it picks up a nut and jams it into a crevice. Using its beak as a hammer, it drums into the nut. When the acorn cracks, she feasts on the meat.

Sometimes taking a moment to observe nature heals what ails you. If there wasn't so much work to do, it would be a fine way to spend time—watching the natural world through the eyes of a child.

After supper, just before dark, Dahlia Jane steps toward the river, tilts her head back, and looks up into the branches of a quaking aspen. The golden leaves shimmer in the evening breeze.

The child reaches her hand behind her neck and points her right elbow toward the treetop. It's an odd thing. It's the sort of movement an older person who suffers from pain in her shoulders might make. After a brief moment, Dahlia Jane turns with a smile and skips to the wagon.

"Good heavens," I mutter to myself.

Rose emerges from the shadows and almost makes eye contact with me.

"Did you see that?" I ask her.

Rose nods.

Usually I don't push conversations with my teenaged daughter, especially since her brief marriage ended tragically. "What in the world was that all about?"

She shakes her head, and replies, "Oh Mama, she does that every night."

"But why? Isn't it strange? I'd like to know why she does that. What is she thinking?"

Rose huffs and frowns. "If she wanted us to know, don't you think she'd say? Who cares anyway?" She shrugs and adds, "What's the harm in it?"

Until I had my own, I never realized just how strange children could be. I should have known better than to ask Rose. Even before she married an Indian on our way to Oregon, she was hard to talk to. Her pregnancy didn't improve her gloomy demeanor. When I start to ask how she's feeling, she wraps the blanket that constantly drapes her shoulders even more tightly. She dodges away, joins Dahlia Jane at the wagon, and helps her sister board.

Though we arrived in the land of milk and honey and filed our land claim, we still camp in tents, and the prairie schooner, like the nomads we have become.

As I follow Dahlia Jane toward the wagon, Pious Bull, Jr. gallops into our camp.

He slides off of the back of his horse shouting, "Dorcas! Come quickly. Serena Bond went into labor and wouldn't you know it, Drucilla Horton did too. Please hurry."

CHAPTER 2

"Oh dear," I gasp. I'll never forget meeting Bobby Bond and Wayne Horton in Independence, Missouri. The two were embroiled in a mighty fistfight. I was afraid they'd hurt each other, so I stepped in and separated them. Over the past year, as we've gotten to know them better, it's hard to think of them as men. They're more like grade school children.

PBJ says, "Ma'am?" It's easier to call him PBJ than Pious Bull, Junior. He's from our hometown back east and I've known him his whole life.

"I was just thinking about Serena and Drucilla's husbands. They must be in quite a state." During our journey these best friends who also happen to be worst enemies had one ridiculous quarrel after another. One time, the competitive duo even brawled over the question of which one would become a father first. I guess it's just about time to find out.

PBJ urges, "Won't you come? Violet's mother and father are both taken sick. They've had the grippe for days. I'm rather worried about them actually." PBJ and Violet Appleyard enjoyed a prairie courtship and a prairie wedding on the way to Oregon. Violet's parents, Hollis and Charlotte, are dear friends and now neighbors. Hollis is a doctor and Charlotte helps with his patients. I miss seeing them, but as Agapito constantly reminds us, life on the trail is different from life on a homestead.

"I'm so sorry to hear that, PBJ. Let's see. Who else is there?"

"Nobody!" PBJ implores, "You've got to come. Violet is squeamish. There ain't nobody else."

The rhythmic tap of Agapito's axe grows quiet.

PBJ notices my shredded dress. "What happened to you, Dorcas?"

I rub my eyes and wonder how I'll make it through a night of delivering babies. Hollis and Charlotte picked a rotten time to come down sick. I explain that a tree fell on me, point at my head, and say, "It sure did a number on me, PBJ."

When Agapito steps into camp, he looks agitated. Normally, he's even-tempered. Finally, he says, "Quick. Think. What are we going to do?"

I reach an arm across his shoulders and say, "I have to go, *mi amor*. What else can I do?"

"Well then," he says. "We will all go. Soon it will be dark. We must not waste time."

Instead of changing into my other dress, I discard my ruined garment. By now everybody knows that I wear men's clothing underneath anyway. It's more practical for riding horseback and lady lumberjacking on the frontier than women's clothing, and I've grown used to it. I may never go back to dressing like a proper lady.

After climbing into the saddle, Agapito passes Dahlia Jane up to me. My old friend, Blizzard, the gentle Andalusian stallion who made the trip from back east with us seems pleased to make a journey this evening as well.

It's a little less than three miles to Bobby's house, and Wayne's house isn't much farther away. PBJ gallops off ahead. Agapito, Rose, and the boys walk along beside me as I ride. I guess they figure it would be too much of a bother to drag the covered wagon along. Christopher carries Paw for his sister, and his dog, Boss, follows closely near his heel.

After about a half a mile, we pass Hollis and Charlotte's wagon. Their cabin isn't finished yet either. PBJ and Violet's camp is a short distance northeast of her parent's place. After riding around a bend in the river and traveling another two miles, we reach Bobby and Serena's place. Less than a tenth of a mile away, a tendril of smoke twists from a stone chimney atop Wayne and Drucilla's small cabin.

I'm stunned.

After traveling with these two young men and all the trouble they got into along the way, drinking and fighting, I can't believe they've already finished building their first homes on the frontier. They're strong boys, but I figured they'd be the last ones to be ready for winter.

When we reach the front door, Bobby greets Agapito with a fast handshake and thanks me for coming. Wayne helps Dahlia Jane down, and when my feet hit the ground, he whisks Blizzard away. It's getting dark and I wonder, have they also built a barn already? I can almost imagine their pregnant wives pointing shotguns at them and making them work around the clock to finish their lodgings.

Inside Bobby's house, I'm confused. "Where's Serena?" I ask.

Bobby's eyes grow wide and he shakes his head. "They're over there. Kicked us out an hour ago." He runs his hands up his face and over his head before holding his hands out in front of him.

His brother-in-law, Wayne, shudders. "They've turned on us. Got downright mean and nasty. Didn't feel right leaving and didn't feel right staying.

Bobby bumps his shoulder into Wayne, and says, "Don't know what we woulda done if you hadn't come, Dorcas."

"Well," I tell them. "You gentlemen better settle in. This could be a long night. I'd best get to it."

Agapito says, "I'll walk you over."

As I make my way through the doorway, I hear Andrew asking Bobby if he has any books or anything to read.

I can't worry about the children now. They'll have to take care of themselves like they did along the trail.

It's Bobby and Wayne that worry me. New fathers are the worst. Nowhere when you need 'em—always underfoot when you don't.

I'm pleased but a little bit surprised when Rose follows me to the other cabin. She's got an awful bedside manner, but she's very helpful with midwifery. I've learned not to ask about the powders, herbs, poultices, and teas she swears by, but they always seem to help.

Bobby and Wayne were right about the urgency of the situation. Perhaps it will not be as long a night as I thought it would be. After asking a couple of questions and examining the patients, I figure Serena will have her baby in an hour or two. Drucilla isn't far behind her. I'm no expert. I've attended more deliveries than I can count, but usually somebody else is in charge. Somebody like Charlotte Appleyard or her husband, the doctor, Hollis.

The husbands were mistaken regarding their wives' disposition. Serena is as pleasant as ever. She's relentless with expressing her gratitude. It's a frightening thing, having a first baby, or any baby for that matter, but Serena doesn't seem to have any fears or hesitation. Thankfully, she too has been present for many labors, or confinements as we're supposed to call them around menfolk.

Between contractions, Serena chatters about one thing after another. First, she talks about how Bobby and Wayne worked together felling trees, stripping bark, notching logs, and crafting their cabins. Then she chatters about our fellow travelers. Finally, she talks about the baby. "We can't decide what to name him. Bobby wants to call him Montgomery Emmanuel Bond. I'm not sure I like the sound of that."

A contraction interrupts her musings. "Whew. That was a rough one. Anyway, Montgomery Emmanuel sounds too highfalutin to me."

"What if it's a girl, dear?" I ask.

Serena turns her head inquisitively. "We hardly ever talk about that. Bobby says everyone in his family has a boy first, before they have a girl." She turns her head and looks at her bedmate. "Dru says it's going to be a boy, because of how it's carrying. And when I dream about the baby, it's always a boy. Dreams don't lie, do they, Dorcas?"

Her dreams must be nothing like mine. But there's no time to debate the foolishness of that statement.

Drucilla has a powerful contraction. The normally polite, quiet young lady doesn't weather the storm like her sister-in-law. It's not the first time I've heard sweet, young girls swear like mountain men at a rendezvous, but I wouldn't have expected it from Dru.

When her contraction has passed, Drucilla whines. "I'm hungry." She looks toward the larder. "I know it's late." She yawns and a tear sails down her cheek. "But do you think I could have something to eat?"

I look at Rose. She shrugs. I suggest, "How about an egg, dear? Does that sound good?"

Drucilla answers, "Oh yes, that would be fine."

Serena interrupts Drucilla as the hungry mother-to-be thanks me, and returns to talking about her baby boy.

Rose has been quiet since we arrived, which is normal. "It's a girl," Rose tells Serena.

"Do you think so?" Serena chatters on, quickly dismissing Rose's prediction, and begins to plan her baby boy's professional career.

Rose adjusts the enormous blanket that cloaks her shoulders. "It's not a boy," she insists.

Another contraction halts the conversation.

The shelves of Drucilla's larder are well organized. I find everything I need and place a skillet on the stove, melt a glob of lard, and crack a couple of eggs.

I don't know what's come over me. Must be the knock I took to the head. And the dizziness. I'm afraid for an instant that I might hork, but the feeling passes. The tumble in my belly doesn't last long, but after these eggs are cooked, I might sit down for a minute.

After a long day of chopping down trees, getting clobbered on the head, and tending to midwife tasks, I could sure use some rest. It crosses my mind to make a pot of coffee, but there isn't time for that.

Serena's next contraction is a strong one. Drucilla follows Serena almost immediately. I've never attended a delivery like this one. It's as if these women are having a competition of their own. But they aren't prone to silliness like their hot-headed husbands.

For a moment, I try to imagine how we'll deliver two babies at once—in the same bed. I'm glad I'm not in their predicament. Before I can hatch a plan to deal with the situation, it's upon us.

Two hours later, each woman holds a brand-new baby girl. I look at the clock and it's just before midnight. These little girls will share a lot together in life, including a birthday. It's almost time to tell the menfolk. But first, I rack my brain. Given that Bobby married Wayne's sister and Wayne married Bobby's sister, how are these baby girls related?

I don't recall voicing the question, but Rose answers, "They're called double cousins, Mama."

"Yes, dear. That's right. I've heard of that before."

If Serena or Drucilla are disappointed by not having sons, it doesn't show. They look tired, but content, as most mothers do when their labors are done.

Rose remains with the women as I scamper through the darkness to the cabin nearby. When I open the door, Dahlia Jane begins screaming. She is asleep on the floor and I hurry to her side. As I pick her up, I wave at Bobby and Wayne. "Mothers and babies are fine. Go. Go to them now."

I clutch Dahlia Jane to my bosom, and Agapito hurries to my side, placing a hand on her back.

"It was horrible, Mama." Her screeching awakens the boys, asleep at a small table, their heads on its surface.

Dahlia Jane sobs, then stops and howls, "What will we do, Mama?"

I try to reassure her. "Hush, child. Everything will be alright."

It's been a few months since she had a night terror like this.

Mother Marten

Well after dark, a mother and four kits slink through the night, sniffing at the edges of camp.

It's not the first time they've skirted the place. The hungry family is drawn to the lingering smells of recently cooked food.

They have been stalking the campsite for weeks. On a couple of occasions, after the people retired into the covered wagon and nearby tents, the pine marten family scurried into camp and made off with discarded scraps and crumbs that the people never missed.

Something is different. Maybe it's instinct. Perhaps they understand that the people's sounds and smells are missing. Somehow, the wild scavengers know this camp is unoccupied.

At first the invasion is tentative. The mother scampers closer. She stops, listens, and wiggles her nose. Nothing.

She slithers closer and turns her head. Nothing.

Ever wary, she inches closer to the center of camp. Her kits follow briefly, but then they fan out. They young martens have matured to the point where they no longer wait to see what their mother will do.

One kit scales the back end of the covered wagon and disappears inside. Another kit dashes through the opening at the front of the covered wagon. A third circles the campfire. The fourth rips a wide gash through the canvas roof of a tent.

The mother digs her claws into a tree, scampers down a clothesline, and shreds a child's dress. Despite being laundered, the garment's pocket still carry the kitten's smell, but Dahlia Jane's kitten isn't there. The mother marten becomes entangled and drags the frock off. With her sharp teeth and claws, she frees herself with a growl.

Nearby, a broody hen in a wooden box pokes its head between the slats. It is as if the bird wants to get a better look at the horrors surrounding her.

The mother marten pounces on the chicken. She quickly devours its head. With her sharp claws, she extracts and consumes as much of the hen's body as she can sink her nails into. The pullets inside the crate are safe, for now.

The mother marten will no doubt remember the maturing chickens and try to make a future meal of them.

Inside the wagon, the pair of kits claw open sacks of coffee, flour, and cornmeal. They tumble around inside the wagon, fighting over the territory, though there's more than either kit could consume in a year. One of their siblings rips a hole in the canvas above them and drops into the fray. The fourth kit tears another opening above. In the wagon bed, the littermates fight among the spoils of war.

The ultimate prize lies safely in a strong, wooden crate. Whatever it contains smells fantastic. Forgetting about their quarrels, the kits begin gnawing on the wood to get inside the box. One of them discovers the lid is not fully secured and claws its way inside, sinking its teeth into a large, salt-cured slab of bacon.

The kit is quickly clawed away by a sibling, and the foursome scramble to lay claim to the crate full of meat. Dislodging the cover, and toppling it over, unleashes even more of the enticing smell into the air, and the mother pine marten hops aboard. The opportunistic family fights over the fatty meat, dragging most of it from the wagon.

Each scavenger feasts on its own private pile of pork until they can't eat any more. The night is far from over. Despite having overindulged, they investigate every corner of the camp, sticking their noses into everything. They urinate on blankets, defecate in the wagon bed, and shred the carefully bagged aromatic herbs and fragrant teas.

Hours before dawn, the heavens open up and it rains heavily for an hour. The soaking rain drenches the campsite but does not wash it clean. In the aftermath of the overnight storm, the spoiled coffee, flour, and cornmeal in the bed of the wagon is flooded with rainwater.

The kits are late to leave home. They've been fit to be weaned for weeks. This night's raid is the family's last night together.

As the sun begins to rise, the mother growls at her young. They don't seem to understand.

She bares her teeth, wrinkles her nose, and emits a high-pitched scream.

Most pine marten kits are eager to move on once they reach maturity, but this mother's kits don't seem to get the message.

The kits are used to tumbling playfully with each other. But when their mother crashes into them with her razor sharp teeth exposed, her claws extended, and ferocious growls, the kits finally understand their destiny. Now, they are adults. Each must find their own territory. One scampers north, another east, the third south, and the fourth creeps westward.

With an overstuffed belly and tired muscles, the mature marten slowly makes her way back to her den in a dark forest surrounded by crowded pines. She drags a chunk of cloth with her, ripped from a child's dress. It takes much more effort than usual to claw her way up the rough tree trunk to her hidden lair in a hollow of the Douglas Fir. She sprawls out within the space that only the day before held four bodies more than it should.

The familiar babble of a creek emptying into the Clackamas River nearby lulls the creature to sleep. The soft moss and cushy leaf bed beneath her provide all the comfort she needs until the sun sets again. She adds the clump of fabric to her hoard and enjoys the smell of the fuzzy feline that rode in the child's pocket. Mother marten no longer has to share her sleeping quarters or territory with her offspring.

If pine martens dream, this mother's reveries might revolve around the pioneers' encampment. It's a mere eight hundred feet away from mother marten.

CHAPTER 3

Dorcas

Despite the late night, Agapito is awake and ready to return home before dawn.

Yesterday was a long day. I'm grateful that all of the scrapes and bruises are surface wounds. The lump on my head isn't as big as it was last night. I'm still feeling a little dizzy and nauseous, but it's nothing compared to last night.

It was kind of Bobby to let Dahlia Jane and me sleep in his bed. The men and boys slept on the floor and Rose stayed with the new mothers in Wayne's cabin.

Bobby offers to make us breakfast. I can't imagine him cooking. It might be interesting to see what he can come up with on his own, but Agapito declines.

"I'll fix us something when we get home," I say.

"Wait," Bobby shouts. He disappears into a small outbuilding I hadn't noticed before. When he returns, he says, "Day before yesterday I shot an elk. I want you to have this roast." He ties the carefully wrapped meat behind Blizzard's saddle and my mouth waters as I thank him.

On the way home, Andrew and Christopher try to guess what the new parents will name their baby girls. Then the children start talking about Christmas. If it weren't for the newborns, I might not know what day it is, but the occasion of their birth requires taking note of the date—November the thirtieth. So, Christmas is less than a month away. I can't help but sigh. I normally welcome the season, but there is so much to do before winter.

Dahlia Jane asks Agapito how he celebrates Christmas. That question never occurred to me.

Last year, Christmas came to us in a small, rented home where we overwintered with fellow travelers from the Adirondack mountains of northern New York before making our way to Independence in April. That's where we met Agapito, the assistant wagon master. I can't recall him ever speaking of Christmas.

My mind wanders as he cheerfully answers their questions in great detail. Good heavens, it all sounds so complicated. I'm not sure if I have the energy for a one day celebration, let alone a nine day event. I don't know the first thing about how to make a tamale or a piñata. With winter coming, and no roof over our heads, who has time to think about crafting figures for a nativity scene?

Christopher's stomach growls and he complains about being hungry. That growing boy is always hungry. As we grow closer to camp, I must admit I'm also looking forward to breakfast. Even pancakes and bacon, our regular breakfast on the trail sounds enticing.

Nothing could prepare us for our arrival in camp. The first thing I notice is the clothesline. We left in such a hurry, we forgot to take down the laundry.

Next, I spy the rips in the wagon bonnet. My heart lurches as I realize that it isn't just torn. It has been ripped to shreds. And then, I recall the storm that passed through overnight. "Oh, Agapito! Everything's ruined." I pass Dahlia Jane to Agapito and dismount.

We wander among the ruins, dumbfounded.

It's impossible to find words to describe the devastation. The worst sight is at the bottom of the wagon bed. There's a couple of inches of water. Our provisions have been ripped to shreds. There's no saving any of it. Flour, corn meal, coffee, sugar, and bacon. All of it ruined. Whatever creatures invaded camp in our absence, the bacon was their favorite.

Dahlia Jane shrieks. The sound is even more horrifying than the one she makes when she gets the night terrors.

I turn to look at her and see her holding her favorite dress, ripped to shreds with a big chunk missing. She points into the crate that holds our chickens until we can build a proper coop. Something has bitten the head off of the broody hen. The surviving pullets huddle together at the other end of the crate.

Dahlia Jane blubbers, "Gloria. Poor Gloria. Just like Gloria." She's talking about the hen that traveled most of the Oregon Trail with us, until she escaped one day and a wolf got her. Several sleepless nights, gory nightmares, and howling night terrors followed for days after that disaster. I know because, strange as it may be, we experience the same nightmares.

And it isn't just the loss of a pet. Dahlia Jane loves cakes, and without eggs, we can't make cake. But our situation now is more dire.

We don't have flour or cornmeal. What will I feed our family? I look at the beheaded chicken and think about whether I can cook what remains of it. We may have to butcher the pullets to survive.

Andrew says, "Maybe we can borrow food from the neighbors."

I just look at him. Nobody on the frontier likes to ask for handouts or accept charity. Then, I remember the elk roast. Thank heavens for that. But what will we do when that's gone?

Finally, Agapito says something. "*No hay mal que por bien no venga.*"

I snap. "You're speaking in Spanish again, Agapito."

Good heavens. I didn't mean to sound harsh, but the bite in my tone even hurts my ear. "I'm sorry, Agapito. I didn't mean it to come out like that."

He says. "It means, there is no bad from which good does not come."

I stare at him. Even in English, I don't understand. He sounds cheerful, but look at the carnage all around us.

Agapito elaborates, "Maybe you would say that every dark cloud has a silver lining."

It's hard to comprehend having an optimistic outlook under the circumstances. "Goodness gracious. What silver lining? What are you talking about?"

He turns away from me and pinches his chin. I've seen him do this before when he's trying to think of something. He shrugs and says, "I do not know yet. We will have to see. Right now, it only looks bad. Only dark clouds. No silver linings."

He steps away and builds a fire in the pit at the center of camp.

What looked like a total loss did not turn out as badly as we thought.

Some of our provisions miraculously survived. There's a barrel full of oats, so I can make oatmeal. The varmints missed a crate full of dried apples and a large bushel of carrots and potatoes. Our jerked meat was untouched, but that's about all we have been left with.

Everything else is spoiled. Even Rose's precious spices, herbs, and teas. Gone.

It will take a lot of stitches to save our clothes and blankets. Whatever invaded our camp seemed to take great pleasure in destroying everything possible.

Gleefully, Andrew shouts, "The newspaper survived."

"Oh, Andrew." I can't help gushing.

Perhaps everything else can be replaced, eventually. The only thing that can't be replaced is Andrew's documentation of our journey. Each day's events were recorded for posterity, and nailed to a post in the center of the gathered wagons. Along the way I didn't get a chance to read every issue of *The Rolling Home Times*, but I know his collection is a priceless keepsake. Someday, when I have leisure time, I look forward to reading them, back to back, as if they were a book. Somehow, Andrew thought to move the newspapers to another wagon, before our wagon was swept away in a river crossing. Now the newspapers have survived this. If only there were a way to make a copy of them in case something else were to happen.

But Andrew doesn't have any more idle time than I do. There are logs to split, fences to fashion, and timbers that need to have the bark stripped off of them.

Dahlia Jane expresses the sentiment, "What will we do now?"

Agapito says, "Do not worry, *amorcita*." He often calls Dahlia Jane "my little sweetheart" in Spanish. "We will hurry and build the cabin so we can be safe. And then I will go to Oregon City and get more provisions, so we will not go hungry."

"But what about Christmas?"

I roll my eyes. It will be a struggle to feed the family every day. Who needs the burden of staging a holiday at a time like this? To soften the blow, I gently say, "Christmas might be a luxury we have to do without, this year, honey. We can double our Christmas next year. How does that sound?"

I should have known better. Dahlia Jane wails. Then she drops into a heap on the ground and sobs. She tries to speak, but I can't make out her exact words. But I do hear her say the phrase, "After all we've been through."

Andrew interrupts. "Oh, Mama. Surely we can come up with something."

Christopher piles on. "We can't go two years with no Christmas."

Rose makes a weird gesture and wanders away.

Agapito says, "We can think of our new cabin as a celebration of Christmas."

"Oh really, Agapito. Now is not the time for being cheerful." Sometimes it's annoying when people try to brighten up a hopeless situation. "Can't you see the children are overwhelmed?"

He turns and faces me directly, hands at his side, leaning slightly forward. "Do not talk to me like this. I am not Larkin." He crosses his arms over his chest and glares at me. This is the first time he's spoken to me in such a manner. "Maybe Larkin did not mind, but I prefer we do not talk to each other like this."

Good heavens. It never occurred to me, but he's right. Larkin and I bickered. It's just what we did. Maybe we were used to it. Perhaps we shouldn't have ever started doing it, but we couldn't help ourselves. Now I'm doing it to Agapito too.

My shoulders sag, and I say, "I'm sorry, *mi amor*. I should have held my tongue. I do not want to bicker and argue either."

Agapito uncrosses his arms and holds out a hand.

I place my hand in his and he kisses the back of it. "And now, I will not rest between dawn and dark. Not until the cabin—it is built."

He may not be worried, but I'm concerned enough for both of us. Taking care of our shelter is one thing, but feeding us is another. I resolve to carefully ration the remaining food. Christmas indeed. We'll be lucky not to starve to death before Christmas.

I look at the old shotgun. There's always hunting. Then I think of the river—and fishing. But that will have to wait.

I despise sewing and pushing a needle through heavy canvas is murder on a lady's fingers. Charlotte Appleyard enjoys sewing, and Rose doesn't mind it either. The only domestic work I like is cooking and baking.

I'm not certain how well the crudely-stitched wagon bonnet will shield us from rain, but it's far better than no coverage at all. Hopefully, it will keep Rose and Dahlia Jane dry.

The tent Agapito and I sleep in was spared, but the boys' tent will take some work. It will have to wait until tomorrow. Perhaps the weather will hold and they can sleep out under the stars tonight, or beneath the wagon if it sprinkles. If it storms, they'll have to crowd into the wagon with the girls.

It's well after dark when Agapito returns to camp. He looks tired, but in good spirits. "You have been busy today, *mi amor*."

It's true. Between the shovel and the broom, we cleaned up everything the best we could. It was such a pity burning the food that could have fed us until spring. All is not well in camp, but at least it looks tidy enough.

Aside from a small meal of oatmeal and dried apples, we haven't eaten to-day. The elk roast has been cooking for hours, and I have a thin, one-potato soup. If you cut them up into small enough pieces and add enough water, it's amazing how far you can stretch them. But without seasoning and spices, it's bland.

When supper is over and the dishes are clean, the sound of the river draws me to the edge of the campfire's circle of light. I gaze out into the darkness and think of the wide river. There's only a quarter moon, but I'm tempted to have a bath.

I'm lost in my thoughts and am surprised when Agapito appears behind me, wrapping his arms around my waist. He nestles his chin above my shoulder and kisses my neck. I'm transported back in time to when he first touched me. It was a moment like this one, at Red Buttes. That was the day I left Larkin's safe—he always dreamed of being a banker—beside the trail. It was also the day I stopped wearing my black mourning dress. I'll never forget the shock of Agapito's arms encircling me on that day, or the look on our faces in the abandoned dresser's mirror that somebody else had abandoned.

It wasn't that long ago, but it seems like ages have passed since then. I turn within his embrace and wrap my arms around him. I prefer a face to face embrace. It was a comfort when he held me like that at Red Buttes, but if we are going to be intimate, I want to be able to see his face. I'd rather not have to tell him so.

Within our tight embrace, I say, "Why does everything have to be so hard? Haven't we endured enough?"

Agapito says, "The frontier has many challenges. But you are strong. Do not be discouraged."

He's right. I've always thought of myself as strong. "I suppose you're right, Agapito. It's just, something has changed. I don't know what it is. It's hard to know what will happen next."

Agapito squeezes me gently. "You said that you like adventure. Do you still like adventure, or should we find a quiet town to live in?"

I can't help laughing. "I do like adventure. It's just, It's hard to get ahead of things, that's all."

He kisses me gently and says, "You must keep the faith. On the trail, miles go by. Life on a ranch is different. Sometimes, it is hard to tell you are making progress. Together we will adjust to this new way of life."

I whisper, "Let's go for a swim."

He protests. "The water, it is cold. It is December now, *mi amor*." I think of the first time we saw each other without clothes on.

Agapito says, "I know what you're thinking. Who can stay in the longest?" That amused look on his face is more reassuring than the words he spoke. *Together we will adjust to this new way of life.*

Instead of running toward the Clackamas River, I take his hand and lead him to the water's edge. We disrobe and splash into the water. He was right about the temperature. We hold each other closely, fully submerged. If only it were summer instead of late fall.

A piercing scream splits the air.

CHAPTER 4

That scream curdles my blood and makes me shiver in fear. I clutch Agapito tightly against me.

Agapito says, "I think it is an owl. I do not know why owls howl like that. But I think it is because they are owls."

I say, "We'd better check on the children." After a mad dash to the river's edge, I shiver as I climb into my clothes.

Agapito scampers after me. Racing to catch up, he laughs and says, "I lasted longer than you."

The wilderness is full of undiscovered frightening beasts. Fortunately, the camp is safe, the children are asleep, and whatever attacked the camp while we were away is not a danger now.

It's hard to believe an owl can make a sound like that. If I believed in such things, I might say it was a banshee.

It has been ten days since something attacked the camp, but we remain vigilant. Whatever it was could return at any time.

Being short of food is a constant worry. We're trying to get by on less. The boys sometimes complain about the watery soup, but we must stretch what we have.

This morning, instead of chopping wood, Christopher and I are fishing in the Clackamas River. But neither of us are having much luck.

Dahlia Jane sits nearby, making nests. She collects dried grasses, then weaves them together into long strands, and then coils the lengths into bowl-shaped replicas. Considering she's only four years old, her creations are quite convincing.

Paw plays nearby, never venturing far from the girl. It's hard to believe the docile kitten is the same animal that we took in almost two months ago. I thought that vicious monster could never be tamed, but somehow the fluff ball came around. Dahlia Jane says Christopher tamed it.

We've been at it for hours, with nothing to show for our efforts. Between casts, I watch Rose scour the riverbanks, searching for something—most likely plants.

Rose thinks the biggest tragedy is the loss of her dried herbs and spices. I think she learned about many of them from Charlotte Appleyard who knows about the healing powers of plants.

Rose claims that she communicates with spirits and that they guide her toward the plants that can help the most. She says she has a spirit guide, the Indian woman called Sacagawea—the one who guided Lewis and Clark to the Pacific Ocean.

It's important to Rose that I believe her, much as she pretends not to care what I think, so I try to believe in spirits for her benefit. Somehow it is easier to believe that Andrew can foretell the future. Dahlia Jane's claim that Christopher talks to animals—and that they do what he tells them to do—is far-fetched as well, but the boy does have a way with them.

I fully believe that Rose's dried plants cure people, ease their suffering, and provide comfort during difficult times. What's more, I don't even question her when she recommends something. I can't stand the taste of her willow tea, but I have to admit that it is effective.

Rose says that her eyesight isn't good and claims that people are blurry, but spirits are clear. I don't know how she manages to locate the plants she needs in the wilderness. Her favorite is sage. Some of her sage survived the destruction, but most of what she collected was lost.

I managed to salvage a collection of seeds. In the spring, I'll plant them and see if I can cultivate the shrubbery that grows so plentifully on the prairies and plains. They're nowhere to be found along the Clackamas River. I know she bathes with it, rubbing it all over her body instead of using soap. She claims it soothes her soul.

She stops, kneels, plucks a leaf and holds it to her nose. Then she gathers clumps of that plant and shoves them into her bag. Though it is late in the season, I'm surprised to see her locating so many useful plants.

After a while, Rose makes her way toward the dark forest of towering pines on the other side of the creek that empties into the Clackamas River. I wonder whether I might have better luck with the creek than I'm having with the river. I tell Christopher to keep an eye on Dahlia Jane before making my way across the meadow to the stream.

From a ways up the creek, I see Rose resting on a boulder. Her bag sits on the ground beside her. She has her hands clasped together on her lap. A modest fall breeze sways the branches at the edge of the woods, and Rose tilts her head from side to side, as if she's listening to a conversation.

I dip my line in the creek. Maybe the fish are smaller here but perhaps they're more plentiful. If I could catch a few, I might be able to cook up a watery, fish soup.

After a while, Rose stands and wanders into the woods. Before I know it, I'm wandering along the banks of the creek, making my way closer to where she was.

At the edge of the forest, I see Rose squatting and looking closely at the ground. From here, I can see what's caught her eye. There's a straight line in the soil, perhaps sixty feet in length. Maybe there was once a structure in that spot. As I watch, she picks up a chunk of something, examines it, and then sets it back down.

Before wandering into the forest, Rose looks in my direction. I wiggle my rod and look at the surface of the water before watching the paths she takes into the woods. Nearly half an hour later, Rose reemerges, and tiptoes back toward camp without saying anything when she walks past me.

Curiosity gets the better of me. When she's out of sight, I hurry to the long, overgrown trough. The punky chunk of wood looks like the final remains of a long-gone structure. Perhaps the natives in this area lived in long, wooden buildings. I set the chunk back down and then follow the path Rose took into the woods.

It's a dark place and it feels like it's part of a different world. A couple of hundred yards in, I can see where Rose must have kneeled. The imprints her knees made in the loose soil are easy to see.

I lean forward and examine a spot where she brushed away the litter on the forest floor. My eyes follow the shadow of an unnaturally shaped lump, and I jump in surprise at the sight of a skeleton. My skin prickles, and I feel as if somebody is watching me.

A short distance from the skull, the dried leaves have been disturbed, exposing a strangely-shaped, unnaturally curved piece of wood. A closer look reveals what looks like the nose of a canoe. Maybe instead of coffins, the Indians used canoes. Near the chin of the skeleton, the soil has been disturbed. It looks as if Rose has dug into the soil and scratched at the dirt with her fingers. Could she have found something there?

These woods are dark and spooky. Just being beneath the canopy of these tightly crowded trees makes me sick to my stomach. When I turn to run, I have a feeling like I can't get away fast enough. I try to convince myself that my fears are just in my imagination and stop, turn to look back into the woods, and then look high up into the branches of a tree. There's a long, rotted wooden structure, shaped like a canoe. Maybe instead of burying the bodies in canoes underground, they bury them in branches of trees.

I blink in shock at the sight of a pair of eyes near the canoe. There's a large, dark, weasel-like creature gazing back at me.

What if there are hundreds of them gazing down on me? Fearful that they might all drop upon me at once, I race back to the edge of the woods.

After all of my years living in the woodlands and thinking of myself as a lady lumberjack, I've never been so frightened in the forest.

I chastise myself for being irrational, retrieve my fishing pole, and return to the riverside.

Then it hits me that this haunted forest lies within our land claim.

While I was away, Christopher caught a modest sized fish. I compliment him on his skills, but it won't amount to much divided among the five of us. It's better than no fish.

"Let's take a break," I tell the children. "How about some oatmeal?"

They mumble agreement. If we don't get something else soon, they may never want oatmeal again. After we eat, I take Agapito and Andrew a bowl.

The structure is about two thirds of the way complete. If they put a roof over the logs they've put together now, it might just be tall enough for me to stand up inside. I try to fake a smile and Agapito says, "It is coming along, yes?"

I step inside the space they left for the door, and look around. At least it is bigger than the wagon. I try to imagine the six of us sleeping in it. I hope the winters here are not severe.

Agapito scarfs down his oatmeal in a couple of bites and thanks me for it like I've just cooked a delicious meal. Then he tells us that we'll need to fill the spaces between the logs with dried grasses and moss. Looking at the huge gaps between the logs, it seems like a daunting task. Waiting until it's colder will only make it worse. "The sooner the better," he adds cheerfully.

It's overwhelming to think of all the work that needs to be done. We haven't got enough wood chopped. There's hardly any food. We should be hunting and fishing, but the fish don't seem to be biting. And now we have to forage for moss as well.

With a sigh, I turn away. There was loads of moss in that haunted forest. I shudder to think that I'm going to have to return to that place. Before I take a step, Andrew says, "Mama, I'm writing a song. It's a Christmas song. Do you want to hear the chorus?"

Agapito says, "Let's sing it for her."

I turn back around and Andrew says, "We've been practicing. We sing while we work. It makes the walls go up faster."

Before I can say anything, Christopher and Dahlia Jane shout words of encouragement.

In unison, they sing:

In this land of promise, where dreams come alive,
We build a home, where hope can thrive,

Through the darkest night, we find our way,
Bringing light, keeping shadows at bay.

When it's over, Andrew asks, expectantly, "What do you think, Mama? Don't you think that will make a great chorus for a Christmas song?"

It sounds wonderful and I'm happy to hear them singing joyfully while they work. But I hate to tell them, I'm just not in the mood. I manage to compliment them anyhow. "Nice job, men. I guess I'd better get back to work. Come along, Dahlia Jane."

Christopher says he's staying behind to help with the cabin. I wish he'd catch another fish instead.

I'm still in a foul mood the next morning. I peek outside of the tent flaps and it's dark—dark and cold. I shiver and retreat beneath our blankets.

Agapito groans. "I guess it is time to go to work." He takes me in his arms and it is clear that he would rather remain beneath the blankets as much as I would.

I say, "Sometimes, wouldn't you like to forget about everything and just laze around. And idle the day away?"

He shimmies closer to me and says, "Yes. I would like that very much." His head inches toward me and just as our lips meet, I hear a loud voice yell, "Mama! I'm hungry. When's breakfast?"

Agapito laughs and says, "Good morning, *mi amor*. It is time to begin our day."

When I emerge from the tent, I'm surprised to see a world completely coated in frosty white fuzz. Overnight, the temperature sunk below the freezing point. Frozen vapors cling to everything and it looks as if a foot of snow has fallen. "My, oh my, Agapito. Just look at this. It's hoar frost, everywhere you look. As far as the eye can see."

"What is this you say? Hoar frost? I never heard of such a thing."

If it weren't so cold or if there was a roaring fire, it might be a wondrous sight to behold.

When he pokes his head out from between the tent flaps, he gasps. "Good heavens."

I know I say that too often. I'm sure he finds himself amusing when he mimics me like that.

I ignore Agapito and ask, "Who asked about breakfast?"

Christopher shouts, "I did, Mama. Sorry. My stomach was growling."

"Very well, Christopher. How about if *you* get the fire going."

He dashes from the tent and gasps when he sees the thick frost. "Mama. It's winter." He slips, slides a few feet, and laughs.

Dahlia Jane stands at the back of the covered wagon and proclaims, "I'm not coming out until spring."

Andrew tumbles out after Christopher, singing a Christmas carol.

I groan. I can see how a frosty world might bring the Christmas season to mind, but I don't want to think about anything except moving into a cabin with a fireplace and a roof. A front door would be welcome also.

When Agapito steps from the tent, he says, "Do you remember coffee?"

My eyes close and I try to conjure the aroma. Many women don't partake, but I have a deep appreciation for the bitter brew. "If only we had some."

Agapito doesn't wait for Christopher to finish building a roaring fire. Before he steps off toward the unfinished cabin, he says, "We will also need stones for the fireplace. Using his hands to hold an imaginary rock, he says, "About this big if you see any."

I'm not sure who he's speaking to. I say, "Logs and moss and stones and anything else?"

"Oh, yes. Clay. Has anybody found clay near the creek or the river? Tell me if you find any."

I shake my head. We'll never be ready for winter. How did Bobby and Wayne manage to get their cabins built so quickly? I wish I knew.

A hare hops through camp and Boss goes berserk. I don't know if it is the Irish setter in him or the Labrador retriever that sends him dashing off in hot pursuit.

Christopher hollers. "Boss, heel."

I guffaw. I can't help myself. It sounds like he's saying *Boss Wheel*. That's what the cantankerous wagon master that led our expedition most of the way to Oregon was called. Christopher named the dog after the man. We came to find that Boss Wheel wasn't as disagreeable as he pretended to be.

After laughing, I begin to cry. I turn away quickly and hope that nobody has noticed.

Christopher races off after the dog.

When we gather for supper at dusk, Christopher is nowhere to be found.

I ask Agapito, "Did Christopher find Boss?"

Agapito says, "Christopher, no. I thought he was with you."

I look at Rose and then Andrew. "Has anybody seen Christopher today?"

Both of them shake their heads.

With my head in my hands, I groan. "Christopher. My Christopher. Good heavens!"

There are a million things that can happen to an adventurous boy of Christopher's age. He's learned a lot about the wilderness. But, accidents happen. Remembering when he broke his arm on the way to Oregon makes me frown. I pray he's alright.

CHAPTER 5

It's well after dark, some two hours later, when Christopher runs into camp. Boss follows closely behind.

Christopher pants, "Sorry I'm late, Mama. Is there any supper left? I'm famished. But I've got great news. I found some clay and perfect stones. But most importantly, I found Boss."

There's something about being a mother that compels one to say something like, "And *that* took all day?" which of course I follow up with, "We were worried sick, Christopher. Surely it could not have taken all day to find that dog."

"But Mama."

I say, "That's enough, Christopher. I don't want to hear it." I cringe as soon as those words escape my lips. It sounds exactly like the words my mother used to say to me. What's worse, I'd *love* to know what he did all day. I'll bet it was better than hauling armloads of moss from the haunted forest.

He hangs his head but glances toward the campfire.

A couple of quick steps bring me to his side. I place a hand on his shoulder and say, "I'm sorry, Christopher. It's not much, but I set aside a plate for you."

"Thanks, Mama."

One week later, our cabin has a chimney, roof, and a door. Just looking at my cookstove makes me want to cry.

I don't know what's gotten into me. I'm not prone to crying all the time. Lately, I feel weepy—far too often. Imagine, shedding tears over a stove.

But that stove has a history. I sacrificed it at Red Buttes to lighten the load so that our oxen wouldn't need to work so hard. Until I married Agapito, I had no idea that he arranged for its transport. That stove rode the rest of the way to Oregon with Christopher's hero, Alvah Nye. It wasn't easy to part with in the first place, and its magical reappearance on our wedding day makes it all the more special.

Come spring, I might look at our little cabin differently, but today I'm grateful to have a safe place for my family this winter. A week ago, I thought it would never be finished, let alone furnished.

There's a pair of bunks on one side of the cabin and a bigger bed for me and Agapito on the other end. Near the cookstove, there's a table with just enough room for six chairs in the middle. Somehow, Agapito found room to include a few shelves next to our bed. There's also storage space underneath.

The only thing missing is the chinking. Even without it, a couple of logs in the cookstove warm us up nicely. In Oregon, we're told, it gets cold, but nothing like it did in the mountains back home.

Good heavens, *this* is home now.

It's a comfort to know that the children are safe and sleeping nearby. I can't remember the last time the whole family slept beneath one roof.

As Agapito and I get comfortable in bed, I realize how tired I am, but I'm not in the mood for sleep. During the day, we have very little time together, and I've come to enjoy a few minutes alone at the beginning and end of the day.

As I nestle in beside him, I say, "You must be very tired, Agapito. But it's finished. You must be pleased."

He flexes his arm and says, "Yes, I am very strong. And your boys are strong too. They work hard. We should all be proud."

"Yes. Very proud."

It's quiet for a minute before Agapito says, "Tomorrow, I go. The soup is getting very thin."

I swat his chest, but he is right.

"It is time to get provisions, no."

I grumble. "I've been trying to make what we have left last as long as possible, but yes. There isn't much left to work with. I wish we could all go."

"Yes. That would be good, but no. I should go alone. I hate to spend even one night without you, *mi amor*, but it can not be helped."

"I know. I understand."

"Do you want anything special from the city?"

"No, my love," I answer quickly. Then, I correct myself. "Yes. Coffee. We need coffee. Good heavens, please, bring home some coffee!"

He raises an eyebrow and chuckles. "So we will live on coffee until spring. That is all. Nothing else?"

"Well, now that you mention it, I guess we need to replace the essentials. But you are the expert in what settlers like us need to survive. Do you remember giving us that list, last spring, in Independence?"

"No. I am sorry. I gave that list to everybody. I must have said bring everything on this list. Do not bring anything else. Is that what I told you?"

"Yes. That's what you said, alright."

"I told everybody the same thing. I do not think I will ever forget what was on that list. Even if I tried."

"So you don't remember us that day? We were just another family to you?"

"No. Oh, no. I did not say that. I will never forget the first time I saw you. I was standing on a box, delivering my speech to a group of settlers. Over their heads, I saw a tall woman in a pink dress step into a muddy street and break up a fight." Agapito laughs. "It was a sight to see, *mi amor*. I shall never forget it."

I shake my head. That was when I met Bobby Bond and Wayne Horton. They were brawling on the street in Independence. I couldn't stand to see them fighting. Nobody did anything to stop them, so I stepped in myself. "You never mentioned it, Agapito. I didn't know you witnessed that. Good heavens. You must have thought I was a brute of a woman."

"A brute of a woman. No. I would never say such a thing. Or think it. I did think you were the kind of woman that can raise strong sons and determined daughters. And I hoped that you would join our wagon train."

"I'm glad we did. I can't imagine having made that journey with anybody else. It was the best decision we made." After a quiet moment, I ask about Agapito's plans in Oregon City. Instead of answering, he asks me about plans for the ranch.

"Well," I answer, "I think Gwibunzi will have a foal in the spring. Blizzard is a stallion in his prime. Our homestead should provide everything we need, logs for fencing, grass for hay and grazing, we have plenty of water, but we need brood mares and a barn."

"Yes. That is what I thought. How much money do we have left?"

"Seven hundred and fifty-one dollars. I just counted it the other day."

"That is enough to buy another stallion and maybe thirty mares. But it would take most of our money to do that." He looks at me nervously.

"You have another idea?"

"Yes. You are very perceptive. I was thinking we could round up wild horses. I know a place where there are many, but it is far. Back along the trail. Maybe three weeks to get there."

"Oh," I blurt. "Yes." I think of Gwibunzi. "Good heavens, Agapito. I love the idea of building our business using wild mustangs. Then we can save our money instead of spending it all."

"Yes. We could save the money. Or we can invest it, yes?"

"Hmm. It sounds like you have a plan."

"Maybe yes. Maybe no. I want to think about it and talk to people in the city. I will tell you more when I know more. But there is much to do. Did I hear you say we must build a barn?"

"Well. I think we'd better have two barns."

"*¡Santo Cielo! ¿Dos graneros? No solo uno, sino dos. Dame fuerzas.*"

"That's what I thought. It's too much, too soon. I don't know what you said, but I can imagine."

"No. No, *mi amor*. If it is two barns you want, then it is two barns you shall have."

"One can be small—just a pole barn with a few stalls. We'll need a bigger barn for hay."

"*¡Ay, Dios mío!*" He palms his face and shakes his head in a comic fashion. "I have much work to do, no?"

I lay a big kiss on Agapito. Then, I say, "Did I express my appreciation for this fine cabin?" I kiss him again and add, "We'll be safe, warm, and snug this winter."

He says, "Yes. You will be warm." He reaches up behind his head and places his fingers between the logs in the wall. "Once you finish filling in all these empty spaces."

I had hoped they would just forget about the holidays. Now, they talk about it non-stop. Constantly.

Andrew writes his first verse:

On the trail, we left all that we knew
With the mountains high and the sky so blue
We carved a path where few had been
With hope in our hearts, we began again.

Christopher says, "I like *Silent Night*." He doesn't say that he prefers *Silent Night*, but he doesn't have to. "Your song don't sound nothing like a Christmas song."

I hate to interject when the children have a disagreement. The injured look on Andrew's face and the urge to encourage his creativity compels me to say, "I think it's wonderful. Make sure to write that down so you don't forget it."

Rose begins singing. As I turn in shock, I realize the other children are as surprised as I am. She grips her blanket over her stomach.

Silent Night, Holy Night
All is calm, all is bright
Round yon virgin, mother and child
Holy infant so tender and mild
Sleep in heavenly peace
Sleep in heavenly peace

Her head tips as she finishes. It's such an odd but touching moment. Nobody says a word until Rose returns to shoving moss into the cracks between logs as if nothing happened.

It's helpful having children of varying heights. While I work above, the children work below, though I know I'll need to follow along where Dahlia Jane has been—to pack the insulating vegetation in more snugly.

Every time I try to change the subject, somehow it always circles back to the fast-approaching holiday. I'm convinced that it's all a part of a plan. The children are conspiring against me.

Andrew is the first to mention oranges. "Do you remember the oranges in our stockings last Christmas?"

My eyes mist over. Though I'm happily remarried, it is hard to face a first Christmas without the children's father. To think, I was married to one man the last time we celebrated the holiday, and now I'm married to another.

Christopher says, "Yeah. I never tasted anything so good as that. Can you just imagine a whole tree of them?" He turns to me and says, "Oranges grow on trees, don't they, Mama?"

I frown at the memory, so different from the children's. Larkin was furious when he found out how much those oranges had cost. He was always far more protective of the family's finances than me. I don't think we said two words to each other on Christmas day. With a sigh, I say, "I've never seen them, but I would guess that they do."

Andrew chastises his brother. "Of course they go on trees. It's not like they'd be underground like carrots and potatoes."

Before Andrew can add an insult at the end of his retort, I ask, "Who needs more moss?"

Our supply has diminished, so I make a quick trip to carry back some more. When I return with a spongy armload of chinking, Andrew says, "What I'm going to miss most, this Christmas, is the turkey. Did you know that there aren't any turkeys out here?"

Christopher agrees. "Mmm. I'm gonna miss them too." He holds a hunk of moss as if it were a drumstick, cups his left hand as if it were a bowl of gravy, dips the pretend turkey into the make-believe crucible, and licks his lips.

Andrew rolls his eyes and shakes his head. "You're a dunker. Always were. I declare."

His brother smiles and nods. "That's for sure. I wish I had me a donut and some milk right about now." He looks at me and a jolt of guilt hits me in the gut. He doesn't say the words, but I can hear him saying that he is hungry, anyway.

Rose says, "Who cares about turkey? You can't have Christmas without maple syrup."

Andrew pipes in. "Oh! Oh, yeah. What I wouldn't give for a big hunk of maple syrup *candy*."

Good heavens. It's not like the children are starving to death. My mouth waters and I realize that I'm remembering the sweet, satisfying confections from Christmases gone by. I wish I'd asked Agapito to see if he could find some maple syrup in Oregon City.

Christopher says, "How about a nice loaf of warm bread?"

Dahlia Jane, who had been quiet until now says, "I'd rather have a cake. No bread. Just cake."

Christopher wedges a big hunk of dried grass between a pair of timbers and recites:

'Twas the night before Christmas, when all through the house
Not a creature was stirring, not even a mouse
The stockings were hung by the chimney with care
In hopes that St. Nicholas soon would be there

"Enough," I shout.

I've had it. It came upon me suddenly. "Alright. We'll celebrate Christmas. I don't know how, but somehow, we will. Okay? Alright?"

The children look stunned. I look away from them briefly and fight the urge to cry.

I grumble, "I'm sorry. I didn't mean to yell. I know how much Christmas means to you." I set a handful of filler down and say. "Let's take a break."

After supper, it gets dark quickly. The children make their way to their bunks as I load a couple of chunks of wood into the stove. Then I draw the curtain and climb into bed alone.

In my mind, I take stock of our remaining provisions. Near as I can figure, if we're careful, we can make it until Agapito returns as long as he doesn't take too long.

Unable to fall asleep, I toss and turn instead. There's so much to do. We've got days of work left, before we're finished, and I'm already tired of chinking. We still don't have enough wood. How long can we live on oatmeal and dried apples? And, goodness gracious! Now I've told the children we'll find a way to celebrate Christmas.

I grab Agapito's pillow and smother my face with it for a moment. And then I breathe deeply. Inhaling his scent makes me yearn for him.

He hasn't even been gone one night, but he can't come home soon enough to suit me.

Chapter 6

After three days of waiting, we hadn't hoped to see Agapito yet, though it would have been nice. I'm rather certain of the date, but confirm it with Andrew who pays close attention to such details. It is December 19th.

It would take a day for Agapito to reach Oregon City. Perhaps he could have completed his business on the second day and returned home on the third. But he would have been hard-pressed to get everything he had hoped to accomplish done that fast. It's more likely that he will return home tomorrow.

When Agapito doesn't return home the following evening, I begin to worry. I don't want to alarm the children, but it's easier said than done. Knowing that Andrew sometimes knows when something bad is about to happen, I can't help looking his way. But he doesn't seem troubled.

The next day is a different story. As we stuff the last bit of moss between logs, Andrew frowns and rubs his stomach. "A storm is coming, Mama."

I sweep my hair up into my bonnet, returning the strays to their proper place. "Dearie me, Andrew." If only there were a way to let Agapito know that bad weather is on the way, so he could hurry up and get home safely. "How long do we have before it hits?"

Andrew holds his arms out straight in front of him, and turns like the shadow of a sundial. I've never seen him do this before. Sometimes children can be dramatic. Perhaps he's just making a show of prognosticating. When he drops his arms back to his side, he shrugs and says, "Hard to tell. Seems like it's a way off yet, Mama."

Changing the subject, he says, "I've finished the second verse of my song. Would you like to hear it?"

"Of course."

I listen as he sings:

Now we build with round pegs and square beams
Each plank in place, fulfilling our dreams
To make a home where our hearts can rest
In the warmth of the fire, we know we are blessed

It's a touching sentiment. If only we had food on the shelves, the words might ring truer.

Yet another day goes by and still, Agapito has not returned. I try to keep my back to the children while frowning, but I can't help worrying. What could be keeping him?

As we finish a meager breakfast, Dahlia Jane says to Christopher, "Tell me that story about St. Nicholas again."

It's the darndest thing. I didn't even know he had a copy of that poem, and somehow it survived the Oregon Trail. Maybe Andrew had a copy of it with his newspapers, which was about the only thing to survive the journey when our wagon was swept away. Now, I'm surprised all over again when Christopher recites it from memory.

Dahlia Jane stops him several times.

"What are sugar plums?"

Christopher answers her quickly before returning to the story.

"What are reindeer? Are they like mules or horses?"

"I don't know. I never seen one. Maybe they're more like elk or caribou. But I never seen a caribou either." He returns to his story.

When Christopher gets to the part where they mount to the sky tugging a sleigh full of toys, Dahlia Jane's face sags. It's a fantastical tale, and she seems overcome with a sense of wonder. Christopher recites the verse:

He spoke not a word, but went straight to his work
And filled all the stockings; then turned with a jerk
And laying his finger aside of his nose
And giving a nod, up the chimney he rose

She interrupts him again.

"That's magic," Dahlia Jane squeals, jumping up and down. "Saint Nicholas knows magic. I love that jolly old elf."

My heart skips a beat. It's touching to see her so excited. It's preposterous, yet brings her such delight. I don't know how Christopher managed to memorize it, but for her sake, I'm glad that he did.

The moment he finishes, Christopher says, "Let's go fishing."

If there's something to be grateful for, it's the fact that we've completed the task of making the cabin airtight. We should return our attention to chopping firewood, but my stomach growls. We need food more than fuel, and the children could use a break. I say, "Yes, let's do!"

Rose grumbles. "I don't want to go fishing."

Andrew agrees. "Me neither."

I'm surprised. I look at him quickly but he doesn't seem sick or troubled.

"I just don't feel like it," he adds.

As Christopher, Dahlia Jane, and I make our way to the river, Andrew says he's going to search for berries. Maybe he just needs some time alone.

"Very well," I say. I can't imagine there are many berries that the bears and other creatures have overlooked.

After six hours along the river, we've only managed to bring in three small fish. The largest is four or five inches long. They won't stretch far, but at least it's something.

We return to the cabin, fry the fish, and when Andrew returns with half a cup full of shriveled berries, the children divide them evenly and eat them without complaint. My stomach growls as I watch the children nibble the fruit. To fill my own belly, I drink a large tumbler full of water.

In a brief, quiet moment as the children finish eating, a strange sound reaches my ear.

"Shush," I say, though the children aren't saying anything.

"Listen!" It's not nearby but it can't be that far away either. "Did you hear that?" It sounded like a snort. "What is it?"

Christopher slowly opens the front door.

"Don't," I whisper. "It could be a bear."

He doesn't listen. Instead, he dashes between me and the door jam and scampers forward a few feet, before stopping, and racing back. "There's elk in the meadow, Mama. Can you hear 'em?"

I nod. His words hit me like a hammer and I break out in a sweat. My stomach soars to think of the possibility. If we could bring down an elk, we could feast for days. "Fetch me the rifle, Christopher," I whisper urgently.

In a whirlwind, I swap my bonnet for the hat I wore on our grand journey—Larkin's old hat.

With a finger at my lips, I tell the children to stay near the cabin. "Be quiet, keep Boss inside, and don't stray. I'll be back, quick as I can."

As I inch closer, I tell myself to be patient.

I try to gauge the direction of the wind and position my approach so that the breeze blows into my face. Moving slowly but steadily, I close in on the small herd.

This could be close enough. I might be in range. But if I could get closer, my odds of success might be better.

The elk don't seem to know or care that I am near. The closer I get, the larger the massive creatures seem to be. They fill the air with strange sounds. It's as if they communicate in a language all their own, mewing, grunting, and barking. It's hard to make sense of the primal sounds, and I'm distracted from my purpose while watching the puffy clouds near their heads when they exhale into the autumn air.

Though it's late in the season, a big bull tips his head back and trumpets toward the heavens. It's a frighteningly powerful yet eerie sound, wild and high-pitched. What a thrill. I blink rapidly and my heart is full of wonder as the call reverberates through the trees. A shiver skips down my spine. I feel as if I'm standing in a landscape painting—a part of the natural scene.

I've never been this close to the massive, towering creatures before. They are much larger than any deer I've ever seen. Their coats are rough and dark. They blend in with the browning grass. Their antlers look almost like giant shrubs or small trees, denuded of foliage at the end of autumn.

The faint glint of antlers, rising above their heads, look like twisted crowns.

I feel very small by comparison.

Tiptoeing closer, one small step after another, I make my way toward the majestic creatures.

Perhaps fifty yards from the nearest elk, the wind shifts, and a light breeze carries the smell of the herd. It's a heady smell, earthy and leathery, and mixes with the rich scent of the forest floor. It clings to the air, wild and raw.

My heartbeat thunders in my ears as I ease the rifle into place.

I'm so close, I can't miss.

Gazing down the barrel, the elk is perfectly positioned, exposing its broad side. I cock the gun.

The wind shifts direction. Their heads jerk up. It's startling to see how synchronized their movements are. It's as if they can sense each others' thoughts.

Something has caught the wary herd's attention. In leaps and bounds they spring from their positions in the meadow.

I'm a fraction of a moment too slow. In desperation, I squeeze the trigger and fire a shot. I'm sure my bullet failed to split the elk's ribs, but I'm pretty certain I hit the animal. Maybe in the neck.

Making my way to where they stood just minutes earlier, I look for signs of blood.

My thoughts slip back in time. It's April, I've just met Agapito, and he's holding a lesson in shooting firearms for the women who will travel the Oregon Trail. When I demonstrate my skills, he calls me Dead Aim Dorcas. He rarely calls me that anymore, and I sort of miss hearing that first nickname. If only my aim were true today.

My heart lurches when I find what I'm looking for. It's just a small rub of sticky, reddish-brown liquid on a tall, dried whisp of grass, but it proves I hit the elk.

I'm wary about getting close to a desperate animal, but follow quickly in pursuit. It pains me to think of the creature dying needlessly and I can't stand the thought of depriving my family of a meal.

After endless searching, I am frustrated. It's a pity. What a waste. I've lost the trail and must abandon my search.

Hours later, I return to the cabin, empty-handed. The children's faces droop and I can't help feeling that I've let them down. A mother should provide for her family. It's an awful thing, having to return with nothing. It was such an opportunity. Thoughts about what could have been hang over my head like a dark cloud.

I hate to impose on neighbors. Though I'd provide them a meal in a heartbeat and without a second thought, I nudge the children into motion. "Let's go visit Hollis and Charlotte."

It's late in the afternoon. They're merely half a mile to the northwest, an easy walk along the river. I say to the children, "We don't see our friends nearly enough." I try to think how long it's been since we passed the Appleyard's place on the way to deliver Serena and Drucilla's babies. It's hard to believe that was three weeks ago. There are so many things to take care of on the frontier, it's hard to find time to visit.

Are the children thinking the same thing as I am? What if we arrive just as Charlotte is making supper for her family? I feel like a common beggar, and several times I think of turning around and returning home to our cabin.

As we get closer, I can smell a hearty meal on the breeze. I couldn't turn back now if I wanted to. My grinding stomach won't permit it.

The children don't say a word. I'm lost in a fantasy as I try to imagine what Charlotte is cooking, based on the smell.

When we're almost there, I caution the children to mind their manners. "Don't beg, and if we're offered supper, don't eat like wild animals." Crisply, I emphasize each word: "Do you hear me?"

They nod and we make our final approach. When Charlotte opens the front door, I say, "I'm sorry, dear, I didn't mean to interrupt your meal." I blush, knowing it's a lie. What's worse is knowing that my children also know that I lied. To distract us all, I compliment them on completing their cabin. When we passed by three weeks ago, they had barely begun erecting it. "You sure made quick work out of building this place."

The welcoming arms of kind neighbors sweep us up. We're invited in. We make quick work of asking if Hollis and Charlotte are feeling better after the grippe. When they ask about Agapito, I try to minimize my concern about his overdue return from Oregon City.

Fortunately, Charlotte has an enormous cauldron of hearty stew and a skillet full of sizzling cornbread. She must have made enough to last a couple of days.

There aren't enough chairs around their table for all of us, but she reassures us, "Eat up. We've got plenty!"

When we return from visiting the Appleyards, I lean against the wall and watch the children. It was humiliating, imposing on neighbors at mealtime, but I was desperate to feed the children.

Rose makes her way to her bunk, cloaked in her familiar blanket. Andrew sits at the table and hunches over a tablet of paper. Dahlia Jane plays with a couple of handfuls of hazelnuts and asks Christopher to recite the poem again.

When he's done, she repeats the names of the reindeer, copying her brother. "Now, Dasher! now, Dancer! Now, Prancer and Vixen! On, Comet! on, Cupid! On, Donder and Blitzen!"

Andrew looks up from his notes. "To the top of the porch! To the top of the wall! Now dash away! Dash away! Dash away all!"

There are just two days left between now and Christmas. Agapito should be home by now. His safe return may be all we can expect for Christmas this year. Even if we can't provide the children a bounty of treasures, we should at least have a meal to put on the table.

I ask Andrew, "Any word on that storm?"

With a grimace, he answers. "It's still coming, Mama. I think it's getting closer, but it's hard to tell for sure."

I frown and look at my bed. I haven't slept well since Agapito left. I'm exhausted. Turning back to Andrew, I say, "Well, I sure hope it holds off. Storm or no storm, I'm going hunting tomorrow. We need meat."

Maybe instead of hunting, I should ride toward Oregon City. Should I ask Hollis and PBJ to make the trip to see what could be keeping Agapito?

As I climb into bed, I think, *A hunter doesn't always succeed, but she never gives up. Tomorrow, I shall ride off into the hills with a rifle and a shotgun.*

CHAPTER 7

First thing in the morning, I look into the heavens. It's mostly cloudy, but the skies don't look too threatening. Andrew is sure that a storm is brewing, but I don't intend to go far in search of game.

I tell the children to stay close to home.

Christopher says, "Can I go to Cobb's house for some goat's milk?"

I frown. Cobb and his three children rode in the wagon directly behind ours most of the way to Oregon. Now we hardly see them. They are our nearest neighbors. When Cobb lost his wife after the birth of their baby girl, we lent him our goat, Ridge. We share the milk. "Very well, Christopher. Yes, you can go to Cobb's house, but don't stay long and don't go anywhere else."

Instead of riding my dependable Andalusian, I decide to ride Gwibunzi, the dazzling paint horse. I can't help thinking of Dembi Koofai, the Shoshone scout who helped guide us to Oregon. He was with me on the glorious day I captured the wild mustang near the Green River.

As I slide the shotgun into one scabbard and the rifle into the other, I think of the four riders that departed almost two months ago: Alvah Nye, Stillman Southmaid, Arikta, and Dembi Koofai. After spending half a year journeying from Independence, Missouri to Oregon City over a northern trail, they return without wagons along a southern route. By now they've probably left California and turned their horses east. If it's hard to imagine celebrating Christmas alone at the edge of civilization in Oregon Territory, it's harder still to imagine Christmas in a desert, surrounded by sand and cacti. And then, four months from now, they'll lead a new army of greenhorns west.

I wave to the children and ride northeast, keeping myself between our cabin and the final beacon along the Oregon Trail. The clouds float high in the sky, and the gleaming, snow-covered dome of Mount Hood remains visible in the distance.

My thoughts return to Agapito. I worried that he would miss his life, following the trail and guiding emigrants. I told him I would ride back and forth with him each year, but he decided to settle down rather than continue riding the trail.

It's hard to think that after surviving, year after year on the dangerous trail, that a two-day round trip journey could keep him away for so long. I manage to convince myself that he will be fine, that he will be home soon, and that by the time I return with fresh meat, he will have arrived with a wagonload of provisions.

Now I can't stop thinking about Christmas. But what can I do? There's no store within miles. I don't have the time or materials to even craft mittens or socks. I've been putting off thinking about it, hoping for a creative burst of inspiration, but I can't come up with a thing. A hearty meal is the only thing I can provide this year. I hate to disappoint the children.

My thoughts drift, and I imagine the wildlife I might encounter ahead. Any game would be welcome. A deer would be best. My thoughts run wild as I contemplate bringing in big game, like an elk or moose. Then that poem about St. Nicholas comes to mind. I imagine one of those reindeer flying through the sky. It doesn't seem right, but I fantasize lifting the rifle and shooting a reindeer out of the sky. That would certainly be a welcome Christmas miracle. It would feed the family for a week.

After an hour and a half, Gwibunzi steps into a meadow that looks promising. At its edge, I see movement. Maybe it's just the breeze making the grasses sway, but I pull the shotgun from the scabbard, just in case an opportunity presents itself.

Riding a little closer, I see another flicker of movement.

There's a trio of partridges foraging at the edge of the meadow. They don't seem worried about my presence. I slowly swing the shotgun into position, aim at the middlemost bird and squeeze the trigger. The firearm bucks violently into my shoulder. The bird I aimed at is down, and the survivors scatter to safety. What a thrill. If I weren't in the saddle, I'd jump up and down.

Partridges aren't very big. It won't last long, but it will feed the family. I wonder, should I ride home now, or save the bird for Christmas?

I gaze at the sky. The light clouds have darkened significantly and have descended. The top of Mount Hood is no longer visible. My instinct tells me that I should return home, but I'd like to bring in more meat. I tie the partridge behind the saddle, reload the shotgun, rub my sore shoulder, mount Gwibunzi, and soldier on.

Another hour passes and the clouds move more swiftly across the sky. Despite the threatening skyline, I push farther on to the northeast.

When the ground becomes marshy, I see a flock of ducks and make my way forward. My heart beats faster, and I imagine bringing in a second bird. This time, I miss. The Mallard flaps its wings and flutters away to safety, taking with it a flock of lucky ducks. I can't help watching the magnificent creatures soar off toward a safer swamp.

Again that thought niggles in the back of my mind. I should turn back. But perhaps there's a herd of elk or deer just ahead. It would be a shame to give up too soon and miss the bounty of such a blessing. And so, on I go, constantly telling myself that I'll turn back after cresting the next hill, rounding the next bend, or reaching the next enormous tree.

My shoulder smarts as it often does when I fire the shotgun. I'm more used to the rifle's kick, which isn't as strong. After firing the shotgun twice, I know my shoulder's going to be sore for hours.

Half an hour after missing the Mallard, the clouds have fully descended. Not even the base of Mount Hood is visible. I've pushed my luck far enough. Now it is definitely time to turn back.

As I rein Gwibunzi around, the wind picks up. I shift in the saddle and untie my coat. Bad weather is no longer a mere threat. Rain is imminent.

With a squeeze of my legs, I prod Gwibunzi from a walk to a trot and then a lope. I doubt it will keep me dry, but perhaps the mustang can outrun the worst of the storm.

When we reach the swamp where I failed to drop a duck, the air thickens. We're completely surrounded by heavy fog that seems to have risen from the ground and descended from the sky at the same time. Due to poor visibility, I must slow Gwibunzi to a walk. It's as though we've been swallowed by the clouds.

The silence is unsettling. What happened to the strong wind? There's something frightening about the fierce quiet. My scalp tingles. Maybe this is how Andrew feels when he gets an inkling that danger is on the way.

I do my best to guide Gwibunzi back the same way we came, but it's difficult when visibility only extends five yards beyond the horse's ears. Maybe it would be best if I don't use the reins to tell the horse where to go. The mustang's instincts are probably better than mine. As long as she seems to be headed in a straight line, directly forward, I let her take control.

There's a sudden, massive drop in the temperature. It's as if we stepped over an imaginary line, going from autumn to the depths of winter in a snap of the fingers. I turn the collar up on my coat and fasten it tightly at my neck. It would be nice to have a thick blanket, like the one that constantly drapes over Rose's shoulders.

Ten minutes after wondering about the eerie silence, the wind picks up and I shiver. My breath becomes visible in the air. It reminds me of the weather in the mountains back home. I thought we had left severe winters behind when we traipsed across the world for the promise of free acreage in the land of milk and honey.

Gwibunzi plods along, but I sit frozen in the saddle. The winds begin to howl and I wonder what might happen next until the first heavy drops of rain plunk onto my hat.

I normally gawk at the spectacle of nature when the sun shines brightly. Being surrounded by the vast wilderness in the middle of a storm is another feeling all together.

The intermittent rain gives way to a constant, drenching gush of water that pours from the heavens and waterfalls over the brim of my hat.

On and on we go. At times, the rain eases up, but then roars back in intensity. It feels as if darkness is descending and all I can do is hope, wish, and pray that the storm will end.

I suppose we're going in the right direction, but how can I be sure when I can hardly see a thing? There are no landmarks. For all I know, every step sends me farther from home, away from the safety of strong walls, and away from the children that need me.

Finally, the rain subsides to a chilly drizzle. It's not dark yet, but darkness can't be far off. I'm just beginning to think that the worst is over when an ear-splitting scream rips across my ear drums. I shiver and wonder what could have made such a sound.

Gwibunzi tosses her head and prances nervously. Her sudden change of pace almost unseats me.

The threat of wolves crosses my mind. I've always been horrified by the mere thought of a pack of wild dogs with massive canine teeth. But the sound we just heard isn't the howl of wolves. I recall descriptions of the sound a mountain lion makes, and the hairs on my arms prickle.

A wave of wild panic washes over me. Oh, how I wish I had turned back sooner. Maybe if I had, I could have made it home before being enveloped by the storm—before being surrounded by the frightening howls of hungry predators.

I never meant to travel this far from home.

The mountain lion roars and I turn my head. It's different from the scream, but certainly comes from the same beast. Only it seems to come from a different direction.

The ferocious creature is not trying to conceal its presence. Why should it? It doesn't need stealth to pounce on me. It's a fright knowing that I'm being hunted. What's more, I make an easy target.

I look for a safe spot to hole up. There's a pile of boulders ahead. I wonder if I might take cover beneath an overhang, but then I worry—is that where the mountain lion lives?

Then I see the cougar. It slinks along a massive boulder, muscles rippling. The flick of its tail, twitch of its powerful shoulders, and its menacing eyes make it look ready to pounce. I pull the rifle from its boot. Should I fire the weapon? What if I miss? I'll only get one chance.

I scream at the cat. Maybe I can scare it away. I can hear the fright in my voice, but maybe it can be fooled. It disappears behind a tree, but I can still feel its presence.

When I reach the outcropping, I dismount. I must be crazy, preparing to camp near a wild animal in the dark during a storm, instead of riding home. But I've become so turned about, I have no idea which direction to go, or how long it might take to get there. These boulders could be my only chance of finding cover.

I drag my canteen, the partridge, my saddlebags, and the rifle from Gwibunzi's back and stow them beneath the rocky outcropping. Despite the raging storm, the ground below is dry.

When I return to Gwibunzi with the intent to tie her to a tree, a crack of lightning illuminates the sky. It's followed immediately by a deafening roar of thunder. As if sensing an opportunity, the mountain lion screams again.

I feel the snap of a twig behind me. Desperately, I lunge toward Gwibunzi and wrap my hands around the saddle horn.

The mustang panics and makes a screaming sound of her own. I've never heard a horse make such a sound before. But I hold on for dear life as Gwibunzi bolts forward. She drags me a hundred yards before I lose hold and she gallops away. Horses are deathly afraid of mountain lions. The storm's deafening howl conceals the sound of Gwibunzi's thundering hooves. But I hear the sound anyway.

I remember when Stillman rode off on a mule, abandoning the wagon train. The fact that he survived a mountain lion attack was truly a miracle. I shudder to think what he must have gone through. He's lucky that Dembi Koofai, the Shoshone scout, saved him.

Now I'm stuck afoot in the middle of a storm, far from home. And a mountain lion wants to devour me.

I scramble toward the rocks where my gear is stowed. There's not much of a fight I can put up. I've got one shot. If that doesn't save me, I could try to club the mountain lion with the rifle.

My last chance and the only other thing I can do is to try and stab it with the hunting knife in my saddlebags. I fish out the knife so I'm prepared, just in case I need it.

Somewhere nearby, that creature watches me. I can imagine its breath on my neck. If it sinks its teeth in me, I'm a goner.

What will become of the children?

What if Agapito never makes it home?

What will become of my babies?

CHAPTER 8

What I feared was nightfall turns out to be just that. I'm hungry, cold, and tired, but I must persevere.

What seemed like a small dry space is actually larger than I thought. There's enough room to pace back and forth, which is fortunate. My feet are numb. Moving helps. When I stop to rest, it seems to get colder.

It would be heavenly to settle into a warm blanket and drift off to sleep. But my thoughts race. I can't stop thinking that this place is the mountain lion's home. As a squall swirls around my head, I try to convince myself that the big cat's den is cozier than this exposed shelter.

I'm not just worried about my survival. The children must be worried sick. I pray that Agapito has made it home.

If only it were Christmas. And the family was gathered around, singing cheerful Christmas carols. And the cook stove was jammed full of firewood. And a fat bird was crammed into a pan. And the hearty smell of steaming stuffing scented the air. And cheerful boughs of greenery hung about, laden with bright decorations. I must admit, I yearn for the familiar comfort of a Christmas holiday now, but my thoughts quickly return to survival.

It's terrifying to think that at any moment, the mountain lion could leap from the darkness, tackle me to the ground, and shred me to bits.

Christopher

Christopher squints, trying to see what's on the table in front of him by the dim light of a candle in an old lantern. The wind howls outdoors and the sound of rain on the roof has changed as the temperature plummets.

With a pencil in hand, looking back and forth from a printed page to a piece of paper, he copies the words to "Silent Night." A commotion at the front door distracts him and he scrambles to see what's causing such a ruckus.

When he opens the door, he's surprised to see Andrew on the ground, moaning. "What happened to you?"

With a groan that makes him sound like a wounded bear, he clutches his stomach. "Don't know what hit me. First I slipped, then I fell, and next thing I know it, my stomach aches."

There's a small, bushy pine tree on the ground beside him. Christopher asks, "What's that?"

"Oh," Andrew's face twists in pain as he makes his way to his knees, "I thought we could bring that tree inside and decorate it." He pinches his eyes tightly closed, leans forward, and hugs his belly. "Something's not right. I ain't felt like this since Mama and Rose got kidnapped at Farewell Bend."

Christopher frowns as he remembers the horrors from that last camp along the Snake River. It wasn't that long ago—just a couple of months, but it seems like years have passed since then.

Rose steps from the cabin and stands beside Christopher. With a scowl, she asks, "What's with him?"

Christopher helps Andrew to his feet, and answers, "I think he's having one of them premonitions. You know, like when he is sure something bad is about to happen."

Andrew's legs wobble but he manages to remain upright. "It's too late. I'm pretty sure something bad already happened. But it's dark, it's snowy, and I can't make out any details. Maybe it's Agapito. Could be Mama. I just don't know."

Christopher looks back and forth between his brother and sister. "What should we do?"

Rose harrumphs. "Do you know where they are?"

Christopher answers, "No."

Andrew shakes his head and grimaces.

Rose turns and walks back into the cabin. "Then you can't do nothing."

Christopher helps Andrew inside and slides a chair away from the table. Andrew drops his elbows on the surface and holds his head in his hands. "Argh. Now my head hurts too."

Dahlia Jane sits on the floor petting the kitten and trying to tie a ribbon around its neck. But the cream-colored cat isn't cooperating with her.

Rose says, "You knuckleheads left the door open."

"Right," Christopher says as he steps toward the door.

Andrew raises his voice but doesn't turn his head. "Drag that tree in here, will ya?"

"Sure." It doesn't take Christopher long to retrieve the snow-covered tree and drag it inside. He stands beside the table and says, "Now what?"

Dahlia Jane says, "A bucket of rocks."

Christopher looks at her and says, "Huh?"

Rose scoffs. "She's talking about the space between your ears."

Dahlia Jane laughs. "No. Stand the tree up in a bucket of rocks."

"Oh."

Clumps of snow fall from the branches as Christopher leans the tree against the wall, looks at his older siblings, and realizes that he'll have to fetch the bucket and rocks by himself. He spins on his heels and dashes back outdoors. Finding a bucket is easy, but it's dark and stormy out. Instead of rocks, he decides to fill the bucket with firewood.

When he returns to the cabin, a gust of wind swirls up behind him and blows the papers from the table to the floor. It takes all of his strength to close the door against the pressure of fiercely blowing wind.

Chunks of firewood clunk against the floorboards as Christopher empties the bucket and decides where to stand the tree. When six people live in a small cabin, there isn't much extra space. He decides to place the bucket near the foot of Rose's bed, just inside the front door.

It would help if somebody would hold the tree up while he piles firewood into the bucket at the base. Christopher looks at Rose, huddled in her bunk, gathered beneath blankets. Andrew has got his head on the table. Could he be asleep? Christopher frowns as he looks at Dahlia Jane. The tree isn't very big. Could she hold it steady?

Instead, Christopher gathers the wood closer to the base of the bucket. The last clumps of snow and ice melt and drip onto Christopher's shirt. He holds the tree with one hand, and packs the kindling in tightly around the base of the trunk with his other hand. When he's done, he steps back and looks at the results. It's a little crooked, but it stands. He tries to shake the tree, but it's tightly wedged. With a shrug, he decides, *That will do.*

Dahlia Jane jumps up and down and claps. Then she points at the puddle on the floor.

Christopher changes into dry clothes and uses his shirt and trousers to sop up as much of the puddle as he can. When he's done, he asks Dahlia Jane what she thinks.

She answers, "It's too plain. Can we decorate it?"

Christopher shrugs. "Why not. Got any ideas?"

She smiles and nods. "My baby bird nests would be good on the tree. And you can borrow my ribbon collection. What can we use for eggs?"

Christopher rubs his chin. "Small. Round. Oval. Hmm."

Dahlia Jane says, "Nuts."

"I guess. Brown nuts. Brown nests. I reckon that'll do."

She says, "Nuts aren't brown inside. Crack 'em."

Christopher says to Andrew, "Could you help with that?"

Instead of answering, Andrew turns his head away and whines.

From her spot on the bunk, Rose grumbles. "Why are you always whining all the time?"

Andrew lifts his head from the table and glowers at Rose. "Why are you always scowling and running off?"

Dahlia Jane empties hazelnuts from her pocket and places them on the table in front of Andrew. Then she brings him a small mallet and a cutting board. Turning away from Andrew, she places her hands on her hips and says to Christopher, "Rose doesn't help."

In a sharp voice, Rose says, "Leave me alone."

Andrew places a nut on the board and whacks it with the mallet. "I swear, Rose. Sometimes it seems like you're not even a part of this family anymore. It's been like this ever since we left home. When was the last time you did something nice?"

"Who does all the wash and mending? It don't do itself, you know."

Andrew pushes on. "When was the last time you *said* something nice?"

Christopher says, "It's like you don't care about nothing. You just stand there, wrapped in that blanket, ignoring everyone."

Dahlia Jane adds, "You never even hold the cat or pet the dog."

Rose stands, wrapped in her blanket with her arms crossed. She looks at the tree, her back to her siblings. "You have no idea what it's like to be me. But how could you?" She swirls around and glares at them. Her blanket falls from her shoulders, and she screams, "My baby. She's gone. Withered away and gone."

Christopher says, "So, wait. Does that mean you're not going to have a baby?"

Rose ignores him. She retrieves the blanket from the floor with a sigh. "I'm sorry," she says, looking briefly at each of us. "It's not your fault. I shouldn't have screamed at you." Stepping away, she adds, "The blanket helps me not to think about it." She returns to her bunk and pulls the blanket over her head.

Dorcas

The storm rages on. It's hard to guess how low the temperature has dropped.

I'm afraid to stop pacing. My hands and feet are numb and my body aches. I'm exhausted, but I refuse to give in. My family needs me. I must be strong.

But it's hard to be strong when that creeping fear tiptoes through your brain. My imagination spins, and I feel utterly alone. It's a struggle to keep the faith. I cling to the rifle like it's my last hope, but with my hands jammed into my sleeves to keep warm, it would be hard to fire the gun quickly enough to save me.

Instead of leaping from the darkness, the mountain lion grunts and pads toward me slowly.

My body freezes in place. I thought I knew exactly what I would do if this happened. I knew it was coming. *Shoot it*, I tell myself. But it is as if I'm a statue.

A thought comes to mind. What about the partridge?

Finally, my body comes back to life. I duck a shoulder, squat to the ground, and grab the dead bird. I hurl it at the mountain lion and scream, "Take that!" Then I say a bunch of words that everybody knows women never utter.

As the fierce animal takes the partridge in its mouth and returns into the darkness, I gasp. *Thank heavens. I hope that monster is satisfied.*

But that's not my only thought. My head is crowded with ominous fear.

One moment, I'm worried about Agapito's return. My children are alone in a frightful storm. And I've thrown away Christmas dinner.

Christopher

An hour after dark, Christopher says, "Mama shoulda been home hours ago."

Andrew looks up from crafting decorations, crinkles his nose, and replies, "I know. I'm worried." He looks at Dahlia Jane before looking back at Christopher. "What if Mama needs rescuing? We should have gone and tried to find her."

Christopher's head tips forward. "We shoulda. But we didn't." He glances at the tree.

Rose emerges from her bunk without her blanket. She scoffs, "Brilliant. You dolts. If you went out searching in that weather, you'd be lost and missing too." She picks up a strand of dried grass and sighs. "Show me what ta do with this."

Dahlia Jane says, "I'll show you. It's easy. Just do this." Her practiced fingers spin the strand together with others, and before long, she's holding a tiny nest in the palm of her hand. "See?"

Andrew gripes, "Why are we wasting our time doing this? Doesn't it seem like there's something more important we should be doing? Mama doesn't care about Christmas anyway."

Christopher shifts his lips back and forth, as he often does. "I don't know why, but I think it's more important than ever. Just looking at that tree gives me hope. Maybe decorating it is like saying a prayer."

Dahlia Jane smartly chirps, "Uh huh. That's right." She pulls out a crate from under the bed. "Here," she says. "Decorate a prayer."

Christopher peeks into the box and pulls out a handful of tiny pinecones, bright hair ribbons, and fluffy feathers. He looks at his little sister then back at her collection. "That's just what we needed. Good job, Dahlia Jane!"

Dorcas

My heart races. I don't know how much more of this foul weather I can stand. I should be grateful for a dry patch of land. I sit, leaning against a hard rock with my knees pulled into the loose bulk of the heavy jacket I had the good sense to bring along.

With my chin and mouth tucked under the collar of my jacket, I blow my breath into the jacket, conserving as much heat as possible. I peer out into the darkness through a narrow slot between the top of the collar and the bottom of my hat brim, but it's too dark to see a thing.

I've got the rifle cradled in my arms. I'd like to think that if the mountain lion attacked, I could bring the weapon into play and not freeze up again, but the temperature has made my body stiff, and exhaustion has slowed my reflexes.

The mountain lion screams again in the distance. My heart races, but I'm glad to know it's farther away than I thought. Hopefully the storm will keep it away, and with any luck, the partridge has satisfied it for the moment.

I shouldn't sit so long. I must get up and walk some more to keep my feet from freezing. If I can stay awake all night, I may have a chance to survive.

Early this morning, as Dorcas rides Gwibunzi on a hunt for Christmas dinner, Agapito departs from Oregon City.

One delay after another has kept him from completing his chores. He never intended to be gone so long. Late last night, he finally got the wagon loaded up with everything they'd need to make it through winter.

Tomorrow is Christmas Eve. Storm or no storm, he is determined to make it home. It's a good thing he brought canvas tarps with him to keep their provisions dry.

Normally, the journey is an easy, seven hour trip. After a couple of days of constant rain, the rough path has turned to mud. The load that should be easy for a strong horse to pull sinks into the muck, and forward progress takes three times as long as normal.

Halfway home, the rain changes to sleet. With each passing mile, the path becomes more slippery and the sleet coats the ground in a thick crust of slippery ice.

At the top of a hill, about three quarters of the way home, the route reaches its peak elevation. While navigating the descent, Agapito's horse stumbles. The wagon wheels slide sideways.

Agapito shouts and reins the horse in the opposite direction. But the load is too heavy. The ice is too slippery.

The sure-footed horse can't hold its ground. The heavily-laden wagon careens over the edge of a steep bank.

Agapito is thrown from the wagon. While in flight, he frantically tucks into a ball and says an urgent prayer before crashing into the ground.

The wagon flips over and rolls into a ravine, crushing the horse as it comes to a stop.

CHAPTER 9

Dorcas

Despite the persistent storm and thick clouds, the sky brightens. The longest, most miserable night of my life is over. Somehow, I have survived but my ordeal has not ended. If only the storm were over. It seems like it has raged for weeks.

I must be out of my mind to think of leaving this spot while the storm rages on, but I must get home. If only I could be sure which direction to travel.

All night, I paced. I'm exhausted and long for sleep but I can't rest until I find better cover. Venturing out into the blowing snow makes no sense, but I can't talk myself out of doing so.

After a small sip of water, I sling the canteen over my shoulder, hoist the saddle bags, and grab the rifle. Instead of trying to decide which way to go, I let the fates guide me.

It takes a will of steel to trudge through a storm. As if I could convince myself that it's a common stroll rather than a desperate journey.

If only the ground weren't so slippery. Every couple of minutes, the weather seems to change, cycling through the possibilities—snow, then sleet, then freezing rain, then snow again.

After many hours, and dozens of falls, it's hard to have faith. My feet are no longer numb. Somehow I can walk on them, but I don't feel connected to them. I shiver uncontrollably and I feel weaker every time I fall down. How many more times can I drag myself to my feet before I am unable to stand again?

Worries and laments swirl about in my head. I should never have left the cabin to venture out alone, especially when Andrew warned me that the weather was going to turn bad. Maybe we shouldn't have traveled across the country to Oregon. I mutter a prayer and frown.

Most of my life, I attended church regularly along with everybody else. In our hometown, the minister was a very kind man. But for some reason, as soon as he opened his mouth and began a sermon, my mind would wander away—not just as a child, but also as an adult. It isn't that I don't believe in God. I do. I guess I'm just a hopeless case. But I could surely use a miracle now.

If only Gwibunzi hadn't galloped off.

If only wild animals hadn't ruined our food.

If only it weren't so stormy.

It starts snowing harder and I can't see a thing.

Lying down and giving up begins to seem like the easy way out, but I think of Agapito and the children. At some point, even thinking about them won't be enough motivation to march onward.

It strikes me that I might walk smack into a tree, but I stagger on anyway.

I whisper into a squall, "Please, God. Help me."

Instead of a tree, I crash into a wall and realize that it is the back of a cabin.

Could I be home?

The ground is even more slippery around the base of the cabin, but I manage to steady myself with my hands on the walls and make my way around the perimeter until I find the entrance. I rap on the door with my frozen fist, but there is no answer. Using the butt end of the rifle, I knock harder, but there still isn't an answer.

It doesn't feel right entering somebody's home without permission, but I don't have a choice. When the door opens, it feels as if God has answered my pitiful prayer. Perhaps I will survive this ordeal.

When I close the door behind me, I stand and let my eyes adjust to the dark gray interior of the cabin. Though it's daytime, it's hard to see inside when there are no windows, and this cabin is airtight.

Just to my left there's a hinged set of shutters. Coming in, I hadn't noticed a window, but perhaps opening it would provide enough light to see what's inside.

Unshuttering the window fails to reveal glass panes. A gust of wind blows snow into my face and I slam the shutters closed again. It's hard to join the clasp. Maybe the strong wind blew it off course, but I finally manage.

Though I can't see much inside the cabin, I can tell that it isn't very big. I inch my way inside. It's smaller than our cabin, and our cabin is modest in size. Maybe this structure is twelve feet square, just big enough for one occupant.

I can make out a bed, a fireplace, a table, and a chair. There are also some shelves near the table, and the wall is cluttered with many objects hanging from pegs.

Shuffling across the floor to the fireplace, I'm surprised to see that there's a wad of paper beneath a teepee-shaped pile of kindling. Setting my saddle-bags down, I wonder if there are matches in my saddlebag, and then I see a small shelf beside the fireplace. There's a small wooden box on it. Lifting the lid reveals dry and well-preserved matches. How convenient!

The tinder welcomes the flame from the end of the matchstick. My body relaxes as the crackling sound of fire snaps the twiggy starter sticks and I add a larger chunk of firewood. I'm grateful that whoever owns this cabin, they have graciously left the wood bin full of well-split logs.

Even before the small fire warms the cabin, I remove my jacket and then my boots. With cold hands, I massage my numb feet. I'm concerned about the color of my toes. Living on the frontier, I'm all too familiar with what can happen to a person's toes if they're too cold for too long.

After an hour beside a blazing fire, I begin to sweat. The small cabin is hotter than a summer's day along the Platte River. With clamped jaws and clenched fists, I ride out the pain of a million pins and needles stinging my toes and feet. Could that be a *good* sign?

Another hour passes and my feet seem to have fully recovered. I turn my socks inside out and hang them above the hearth and remember Christmas. I've lost track of time. Is that today? I'm pretty sure it's tomorrow.

I place my boots near the fire, not so close that they might melt, and tip them over. Hopefully the fire's warmth will warm and dry out the interior of my footwear.

The glow of the rollicking fire provides enough light to see within the cabin. The first thing that catches my eye is a lantern on the table. When the candle inside is lit, I'm able to make out more of my surroundings.

Now that I'm warm and comfortable, I find myself curious. Who built this cabin? Where are they now? I feel like an intruder as I begin to explore, but I can't help myself.

First I make my way around the cabin, looking at the walls and the objects hanging from them. Most of what I see are very useful things. At first glance, it looks like a disorganized mess of unrelated objects, but closer examination shows a more orderly collection of things a person might need or would find useful living in the wilderness. The objects on display say a lot about the person who must have built this cabin: snow shoes, traps, hatchets, axes, shovels, rope, blankets, trousers, shirts, and so on.

The bed is neatly made and covered with a scratchy, Hudson's bay blanket. I run a hand over it, and try to imagine the comfort provided by an object with such a coarse texture. It's frayed and threadbare in spots. I can only imagine the industrious mountain man who carried that blanket and the adventures that he had.

Taking another look at the fireplace, it's amazing to see the careful attention to craftsmanship. It's almost as if every stone is identical in size, and forged to fit perfectly together to form a hearth and chimney.

Earlier, I hadn't noticed the surface of the table where I found the lantern. Now, I see a stout lead pencil and a piece of paper, perhaps more than one. I slide the well-made, homemade chair away from the table and sit down. The seat is surprisingly comfortable.

The handwriting on the paper is tidy. As a young boy, this future trapper must have dutifully practiced his cursive writing, perhaps in a one room schoolhouse. It's a letter, and it is dated. I blink as the date registers: July 3, 1848. To think, this piece of paper has sat on this table for a year and a half.

I read slowly, taking it in, and try to imagine the person who wrote this letter and the life that they led. It says:

To whoever finds this place,

If you're reading this, you've stumbled upon my lil ol' hideaway here in the woods.

I've decided it's time to pack up and head back to Concord. Gonna take another stab at livin' a civilized life, though I can't say I'm lookin' forward to it much. Figure I can find a fussy niece back there who might be happy to pamper an ol' trapper like me with some fine vittles.

The years out here have been mighty kind to me, but my ol' bone sack's grown weary. The ol' joints ain't what they used to be. I suppose these aches and pains just come with age.

I've left a few things behind in that trunk o'er there. Been workin' on that nativity set more years than I'd like to count. Ridden out many a storm whittlin' away on chunks a wood. Whoever you are, I figure the hand a God brung ya. Hope them little statues bring you as much joy as they did me. If it were up to me, I'd celebrate Christmas year-round.

Make yourself to home and he'p yourself to anything ya need. Don't reckon I'll be back this way again, but ya never know. These woods round here have a way of speakin' to ya, if you be willin' to listen.

In case I do decide to return, leave me a note and let me know you stopped by. It'd tickle me to hear from ya.

What a sentimental ol' coot I've become. Do forgive my ramblin' blatherins. I assure you, I'm really rather cantank'rus by nature.

Yer host,
Nicholas "Crabapple" Pike

I look away from the trapper's letter. A shiver of goosebumps washes across my shins. I can just imagine a bearded old mountain man who calls himself Crabapple, thinks he's cantankerous, but is really a kind and thoughtful man. Reminds me of Boss Wheel. I'll bet Crabapple Nick's fussy niece is glad to make a place for him in her home.

When I see what's printed on the second page, the goosebumps spread across my entire body, and I'm overcome with emotion. I have to set the paper down until the tears clear from my eyes before I read it again. In neatly printed, boxy-shaped letters that I would recognize anywhere, it reads:

Dear Crabapple Nick,

Thank you for the gift.

We had to give up Christmas this year on account a we got nothing.

My family will think itz a miracle. I guess maybe it is. Lets not tell 'em otherwise. I figgure you can keep a secret. Specially cuz you ain't here.

I don't believe you ar cantank'rus 'tall. You are too kind fur that.

Your friend,
Christopher

I cover my mouth and turn my head away. Christopher was here. He found this cabin and didn't tell anybody. Then I remember the day he chased after Boss. That must have been the day he discovered Crabapple Nick's cabin.

Strange, I hadn't noticed the chest earlier, but I make my way over and open it. I don't see the nativity figures he wrote about. I clasp my hands beneath my chin. Christopher must have taken them with him. I'd sure like to see that nativity scene.

I squat and see books full of neatly scribed, hand-written pages. I wish I had the time to read more. Good heavens, just imagine, they must contain the story of Crabapple Nick's adventures in the wild mountains. It's hard not to feel a deep connection to this man I've never met. As I close the trunk, it occurs to me that if it weren't for his cabin, I'd probably have frozen to death by now.

Beneath Nick's table, there's a small, round rug. I look at it more closely and try to figure out whether he made that too. When I lift the corner, I realize that there's a trap door underneath the rug.

I can't help myself. I must see whatever else there is to see.

With a shove, I slide the table and chair across the floor. There's a slight indentation in the wood, and with a finger, I pry open the door.

A rope ladder descends into a small cellar. The opening is just wide enough for me to fit through, and the rope ladder is hard to navigate while carrying the lighted lantern.

When I reach the bottom of the ladder, I realize that the mountain man must have been short. I'm forced to bend my knees and hunch my shoulders.

It smells musty and stale.

Ahead of me, there are neatly organized shelves containing small barrels and tiny crates. As I make my way forward, spiderwebs stretch across my face and cling to my hair. The urge to sweep them away with both hands almost causes me to drop the lantern.

Another step forward reveals the dried husk of a huge snakeskin, lying coiled in a corner. Two feet away, a small skeleton with a fierce looking skull and sharp, white teeth makes me think of whatever creatures shredded our provisions.

When I reach the shelves, I can see that the boxes, barrels, and crates are well-labeled—perhaps using the same fat, lead pencil Nick used to write his letter. The labels reveal the contents: jerky, crackers, fruit, nuts.

There's evidence of gnawing on the wooden containers. But the mountain man's packaging kept out the scavengers. My stomach growls. Is it possible that the food Nick socked away is still edible?

I shove a box each of jerky, crackers, fruit, and nuts through the opening and climb back up into the cabin. It takes some doing, but Nick has left plenty of tools with which to open the containers.

It's a miracle. The jerky is well-preserved. The hardtack is stale, but edible. The hazelnut shells are brittle, but the nuts inside are sweet and buttery. The dried berries, a mixture of salal, huckleberries, and elderberries, are shriveled and hard to look at. The texture isn't pleasant, but they're sweet and flavorful. Crabapple Nick's food stores are a Godsend.

As I close the trap door and slide the table back into place, there's a strange tapping sound on the door. It sounds like the rap of a woodpecker. It reminds me of Dahlia Jane's favorite bird, and I quickly return to reality. It's as if I've been living in a dream world.

I must get home at once.

When I open the door, I'm met with a blast of cold wind. Snowflakes swirl into the cabin. I'm surprised to see the woodpecker that made the tapping sound. What's this bird doing out in a storm? It should be hunkered down inside the trunk of a tree, in its nest.

Urgently, I turn back into the cabin. I fill my saddlebags with as much of Nick's provisions as I can carry. I strap on my boots and the mountain man's snowshoes.

After a final look around the cabin, I blow out the candle and leave the fire to burn itself out in the hearth. As I make my way toward the door, I hear the tapping sound of the woodpecker again. When I open the door, it spreads its golden wings and flaps off into the storm.

I can't tell one direction from another, but I must find my way home before dark. I can't spend another night away from home. At the same time, I feel a strong tug of regret about leaving the comfort of a warm fire in the cozy cabin.

When one is lost, one direction is as good as another. So, I shrug and set out in the same direction as the golden woodpecker.

It takes hours clopping on snowshoes through the relentless storm, and every time I feel as if it's hopeless, the magical bird reappears. It flaps its wings and then flies off again. I follow.

It's almost dark again when I reach the front door of our cabin. Andrew flings the door open and shouts, "I knew you would come. I just knew it. I wasn't sure until this morning, but then I seen you in my head, following some bird home."

"Oh, Andrew." I'm so relieved to see him. I wrap my arms around him and hug him so tightly he begs me to stop. I'm more careful with Christopher and Dahlia Jane.

Even Rose hugs me. It's not a full embrace—more like arms on arms.

I'm grateful to be reunited with the children, but I can't help frowning. I want to cry, but I hate to say the words I have to say. "Where's Agapito? Did he make it home yet?"

In unison, they answer. "No."

Andrew adds, "I'm sorry, Mama."

Christopher tries to change the subject. He says, "Look, Mama. Look what Bobby brought for Christmas dinner."

There's a dead snow goose on the table. It's a grisly sight, and yet I know the children are hungry. I look at the carcass longer than I should. I taste the bile on my tongue and feel my stomach begin to wretch. As I dash through the door to heave, it hits me.

Good heavens. I'm pregnant. My moods, the tears, and my unsettled stomach. It all adds up to one thing. A baby. Dearie me!

When I come back inside, Christopher says, "Bobby brought the goose. He wanted to tell you the new babies' names. Agnes and Annabelle. Agnes Horton and Annabelle Bond."

It's late at night on Christmas Eve. The children have gone to bed. Agapito still isn't home. Where can he be? He's been gone for eight days. It crosses my mind to hope that he's in jail. At least then, he'd be safe and warm. But who would arrest Agapito?

A million things go through the mind when a loved one is delayed.

I look at his pillow where his head should be.

The relentless storm pelts the roof and walls, but it's warm beneath the blankets in the cozy cabin that Agapito built. I thought Oregon was supposed to have a mild climate.

After no sleep last night, I can't help drifting off to sleep despite fearing that Agapito has met a tragic end.

Agapito

A thickly-robed, elderly Clackamas woman leads Agapito through the snow. He drags a heavily-laden, makeshift sleigh that looks like a raft. It's crudely constructed from roped together, wooden boards.

The night is dark and the snow is deep. At best, the freight moves at a pace of less than half a mile per hour.

At every other step, Agapito's feet punch a hole through the snow and he must labor to pull his foot from the hole to take another step.

The elder at his elbow whispers encouragement into his ears. He can feel her grip on his arm, but she doesn't help tug the rope.

CHAPTER 10

Dorcas

An hour before dawn, the door opens and slams shut.

I jump from bed, suddenly awake. The children leap from their bunks and stand behind me.

Agapito shivers, moans, and collapses into my arms. "I am so glad to be home, *mi amor*. Oh, how I've missed you."

A gust of wind chills the cabin, and clumps of snow fall from his clothes onto the floor, but I don't care. I shout his name, shrieking with joy and making a fuss over his return, peppering his face with frantic kisses.

As if suddenly remembering his companion, he breaks away. "I am sorry, friend. I do not remember your name."

Before she can answer, I maneuver the door closed as the family crowds together in front of the fireplace. Andrew puts a couple of logs on the hearth and Christopher lights the lantern.

She says, "I am Illahee." She looks old and frail, yet has pretty, silver hair and a warm expression on her face. It's hard to believe that she rescued Agapito, but I'm grateful and relieved.

I bow as I reach my hand forward. "I am pleased to meet you, *Illahee*." I try to say her name as she did, "Ill-AH-hee. That's beautiful. Does it carry a special meaning?"

"Yes. It means *homeland*. This was our home. We lived here for many years. Before we moved north."

I have the same feeling as when I entered Crabapple Nick's cabin, until I saw his welcoming note. As if she can read my mind, Illahee says, "We are glad you are here. Be good to the land." She leans her head forward and joins her hands together in front of her. She adds, "Honor the place where the creek joins the river. My husband was buried there."

Stammering, I say, "I'm sorry, so sorry, Illahee. It is hard to lose a husband." I take Agapito's hand in mine. it was frightening to think I could have lost a second husband. His hand is cold, but holding it warms my heart and makes me feel safe.

Slowly she extends an arm in the direction of what I have been calling the haunted forest. She says, "Thank you. We were very young and it was many years ago. Maybe soon, we will be together again."

Andrew gasps. We turn at the interruption and follow where he points. Displayed on a shelf is a collection of small figurines, varying in size from two to five inches tall. I glance at Christopher.

He shifts his lips from left to right and back again, and gazes at the ceiling. "It's a miracle," he mumbles.

I turn away from him and smile. "Yes, indeed it is," I say. He need not know that I am in on his secret.

As if we weren't beside him, Andrew says, "There's an angel and a shepherd, three wise men, a star of Bethlehem, Joseph, Mary, and baby Jesus. Oh, and look at that. It's Hardtack."

That's just what I was thinking. Of all animals to include in a nativity, Crabapple Nick had to carve an ox. Remembering the dutiful oxen, the one we called Hardtack—the one that led the team as it hauled our covered wagon most of the way to Oregon—makes me emotional. Again. A sure sign that a baby is on the way.

Dahlia Jane claps her hands and jumps up and down. "Look at the tree. Look at the tree! It's beautiful, Rose."

Last night before bed, I had the chance to look at the children's handiwork. The bushy boughs laden with Dahlia Jane's bird nests, hazelnut eggs, colorful feathers, bright ribbons, and tiny hemlock pinecones, were a splendor to behold. Rose must have added the vibrant red rose hips in the middle of the night.

Dahlia Jane tips her head back, points her right elbow skyward, and stretches. Things are happening so quickly, but we just woke up. I could use a good yawn and stretch myself.

There's a strong smell of sugar in the air, and the buttery, nutty smell of toasted nuts—hazelnuts.

When we turn away from the tree we see a tall, iced cake on the table, festively adorned with chopped nuts. I'm astonished. "Where did this cake come from?"

I look from one child to the next. Rose smiles and shrugs. She doesn't smile often. Rose knows something, but I know better than to pelt questions at her. The boys clearly have no idea. Dahlia Jane can't contain her delight. "It's cake, Mama. A Christmas cake."

Agapito shrugs when I look at him, but where else could the cake have come from? We have no flour, no sugar cones, and no eggs.

Suddenly, I remember our guest. Spinning around, I say her name. "Illahee. Where did you go?" My family looks as confused as I feel.

Were we so caught up in the magic of Christmas, with the nativity, rose hips, and a mysterious cake, that we failed to notice her departure. When I open the front door, early morning sunshine brightens a world that had been shrouded in storm clouds and heavy precipitation for days. Clean, white snow glistens and it appears almost heavenly, rather than dangerous.

The roughly constructed sleigh is right in front of our cabin. The deep trail that it carved in the landscape stretches as far as the eye can see. Where human footprints are visible, there is one set of footprints. Not two.

I look at Rose. She whispers so that only I can hear her. "She is a spirit, Mama."

Nobody says anything, but Andrew begins to sing. It's the song that he wrote while helping Agapito build the cabin. In between verses, the family joins him on the chorus, shoulder to shoulder like townsfolk caroling at the front door. We've heard the song enough to know those lines quite well:

In this land of promise, where dreams come alive
We build a home, where hope can thrive

Through the darkest night, we find our way
Bringing light, keeping shadows at bay.

Moments after Andrew's song is done, Christopher tips his head back and recites the poem, naming the reindeer and the visit from Saint Nick. Instead of picturing a rosy-cheeked elf, I imagine a bearded old trapper who fancies himself to be cantankerous.

When Christopher is done, Dahlia Jane says, "Let's have cake for breakfast."

Agapito laughs. "I think that is a fine idea, *amorcita*."

We may not have much food, but we have goat's milk.

Andrew slices the cake while Dahlia Jane squeals and Rose pours milk into shallow cups. Christopher licks his lips and seats himself quickly.

Agapito is almost as fast. "I am famished," he admits.

Despite having eaten at Crabapple Nick's cabin, I'm surprised to realize how hungry I am. Nobody says much as we gobble the buttery, nutty cake. Andrew laughs at Christopher, points, and says, "Dunk."

Christopher pops a soggy bite of cake into his mouth and says, "What?" with his mouth full.

Andrew says, "I swear, we should call you Dunk instead of Christopher. You're always dipping. Biscuits, bread, and now cake. If we don't call you Dunk, how about Soggy?"

Christopher sneers. "If you must, I'll answer to Dunk." His sneer turns into a smile. "Not Soggy." He shudders at the thought.

Agapito pats his stomach. "That hit the spot. Now, who wants to help me unload the wagon?" He grimaces but doesn't pick a different word. The wagon isn't a wagon anymore. "I have gifts for the children." Then he looks at me. There's a touch of sadness in his expression. "I am sorry, Dorcas. For you I have only my heart, *mi amor.*"

My heart skips a beat and I place my hands on my chest, just beneath my chin. "I'm delighted that you have something for the children, my love. I'm sorry I don't have gifts for anybody this year."

I think of the baby that I am convinced I'm carrying. Is that not a Christmas gift for the family? I decide not to mention her.

Rose says, "Him."

I blink fast. It's as if she can read my mind. I think of her Indian husband, Snarling Wolf, who didn't just claim to read minds. He demonstrated it. I repeat, "Him?"

Rose nods and I look away.

Andrew and Christopher scurry from the cabin. Agapito and I step outside and watch as they make fast work of untying the canvas, covering the cargo. I'm amazed at how much is piled on the boards. I turn my head and look at Agapito, "You dragged all of that?"

The corners of his mouth turn up. I've loved that playful smile as long as I've known him. He says, "I am very strong, no?"

I nod in quick agreement. "Yes, very strong. What happened to the wagon?"

He shakes his head and frowns. "It was bad. Very bad. I will tell you later."

The provisions he has brought will keep us from starving. They won't last all winter, but we can worry about that later.

Agapito steps forward and picks up a heavy sack with twine tied around its throat. "This is what I am looking for." He carries the sack inside and sets it on the table, beside what's left of the cake.

His fingers struggle to untie the tight knot. The children look on. I can see the blaze of excitement burning on their cheeks. Even Rose seems attentive. It occurs to me that he is only pretending to have difficulty untying the knot. How dramatic.

The gifts are wrapped in plan paper and tied securely with thin twine. He passes the first package to Dahlia Jane. "This is for you, *amorcita*."

She tears into the package, and howls at the sight of a woman in a witch's hat riding a goose as if it were a horse. I lean forward, read the title, and say it out loud. "*Mother Goose's Melody*. Aww."

"Let us see here now," Agapito digs into the sack. "How about some action and adventure for Andrew and Christopher."

Andrew is polite, but can't contain himself. "I've been starving for something new to read." He tips his head in gratitude and thanks Agapito.

"You have not already read *Robinson Crusoe*, have you?"

Quickly, he says, "No. No. I haven't."

Christopher opens his book, thanks Agapito, and looks at me, blinking. I know what he's thinking. He's told me before that books are boring.

Agapito says, "I think you will like it."

I look at the title. *"Swiss Family Robinson."* I haven't heard of that one.

Politely, Christopher says, "Thank you, Agapito." He opens the book and reads a couple of sentences. Then he picks up the book and retreats to his bunk.

Agapito fishes a package from the bottom of the sack. "This is for you, Rose."

She tentatively takes the wrapped book and looks at the cover. She reads the title out loud. *"The Pilgrim's Progress."*

Agapito says, "You may like it, you might not. Maybe you will like some of it."

Rose clutches the book to her chest. It almost doesn't matter if she enjoys reading it or not, but she seems to appreciate that he brought her something.

"Aha," Agapito says. "I have one more package in the sack. It is for the family. For Christmas. Who would like to open it?"

Dahlia Jane jumps up and down. "Me, me. I will do it."

She yanks the string and tears the paper away before anyone has a chance to object or challenge her. "What does it say?" she asks.

Agapito answers, *"A Christmas Carol."*

"Oh," Dahlia Jane says. "Do we know that one, Mama?"

"Yes, child." I answer. "But maybe you don't remember. We read it together the year before last. But we had to leave our books behind." I look at the older children. Surely they must remember. "We used to read that together every Christmas."

I sniffle and feel the twinge of tears beginning to form. I wrap my arms around Agapito, kiss him briefly, and melt into his arms. I whisper, "Thank you for Christmas, my love."

We have our big meal for supper instead of dinner. I've always enjoyed cooking, and it takes most of the day to prepare a plentiful meal after having so little to feed the family over the past several weeks.

When I'm done cleaning up, I watch as the children file off to bed with their books, but it's too dark for them to read.

My spirit soars to see the satisfied look on Agapito's face. Perhaps new books at Christmas will become our new tradition. I think of Arikta, the Pawnee scout from the wagon train, and the influence Agapito had on that young man.

With my head tipped forward, I say a brief prayer. "Oh Lord, please watch over our friends, so far away. Especially the young men on their way back to Independence, Missouri. Merry Christmas, Alvah Nye, Stillman South-maid, Arikta, and Dembi Koofai, wherever you are."

Agapito takes my hand. He draws the curtain closed, near the foot of our bed. "Amen," he adds.

He dresses for bed quickly, but I take my time, stopping to brush my tangle of hair.

It chokes me up to admit it, but I confess, "I thought we could skip celebrating Christmas this year."

I set down the brush and look at Agapito. "But you and the children convinced me otherwise. I came to realize that the children need to celebrate Christmas, now more than ever. But even then, I was mistaken. The miracles we've witnessed *this* Christmas made me realize that Christmas is for *everyone*. Not just children, but adults too. Not just believers, but doubters as well. Even non-believers, because you never know—you never know when a non-believer might become convinced."

I crawl beneath the covers and nestle in beside Agapito. "Now, tell me about Oregon City. What kept you away for so long?"

He stretches his head back and gripes, "*Dios mío!* Dorcas, you would not believe everything that happened." He tsks a few times and then he's quiet.

Sometimes he enjoys building suspense and creating intrigue. So, I say, "Tell me, Agapito."

He runs through everything fast. From his tone of voice, I can tell how impatient he was with the entire experience. He says, "On my way there, a wagon wheel broke. I stopped to repair it. Then a mile later, another wagon wheel broke. So I had to camp for the night. The next day, I came upon a bear in the middle of the path, and he would not move. He just sat in the middle of the path. I waited and waited. It took me three days just to get to Oregon City."

"Oh, Agapito. What bad luck."

"Yes." He rolls his eyes and waves his hands. "I think that bear was laughing at me. But the return trip was worse." He shudders. "All ice. The wagon—it slid and flipped and crushed the horse. I will have to go back and see if I can save anything else. And when I got to the city everything was closed. There was a sign on every door. There was some funeral out of town. I thought I would be stuck in Oregon City forever. You do not know how happy I am to be home." He blows air through his lips.

I pat his harm. "I'm glad you're home too."

I tell him about my ordeal. "We've seen our share of hardship, but we've been blessed with miracles too." I think of the golden woodpecker, and Crabapple Nick's cabin, but decide not to tell Agapito about the cabin. Let Christopher keep his discovery a secret. I smile at the thought of the nativity scene. Maybe it doesn't qualify as a miracle, but I say it out loud as if beginning a list. "The nativity scene...."

Agapito adds, "And Illahee, the Clackamas Elder. If it were not for her, I do not know if I would have survived."

"Yes, thank God for Illahee, Agapito." I smile and tickle his ribs. "And that cake. I don't know how you pulled off *that* Christmas miracle. But you sure made Dahlia Jane happy."

He caresses the back of my neck and pulls me close for a kiss. "I do not know anything about the cake. It was not me. You will have to look somewhere else to solve that mystery. But adults who will allow children to eat cake for breakfast, that is a miracle."

Somehow the children must have squirreled away some sugar, flour, and an egg away for a special occasion. An occasion such as Christmas. I've been baking for ages, but would never have thought to add hazelnuts to a cake.

I sigh. As the air slowly passes between my lips, I realize how content I am. I'm also grateful that Gwibunzi found her way home shortly after I did.

Life on the frontier isn't easy, but every so often, there are moments like this. I can't think of a better moment to tell Agapito about another Christmas miracle, for after all, isn't every new life a miracle of sorts?

I hesitate for a moment. It took Agapito years to get over the loss of his first wife, Merced, and their baby girl, Sarita. Since then, he's helped Arikta and Dembi Koofai find their way into adulthood as wagon train guides. And my children love him too. I say, "Agapito, do you remember when we met and talked about our dreams?"

"Yes, of course."

"And you said you were in between dreams?"

"Yes, and you will remember when we married, I told you I was not in between dreams anymore."

"I remember. That's why I said yes when you asked me to marry you. I hope you do not have any regrets, Agapito."

"Regrets? No. I do not have any regrets."

"But what about dreams, Agapito? What are your dreams now?"

He rolls from his side to his back and looks above us. "I do not know." He's slow to speak, as if giving voice to new thoughts. "I used to live for the trail. Endless journeys. Helping people realize their dreams. Now I want to build things. Like our cabin. Our life together. Your horse ranch. A freight and stagecoach company. A town. We could start a town near here, no? We have a lot of building to do. That would keep us busy, yes?"

I laugh in his ear and rub his cheek. "Do you think we can accomplish all of that?"

"Maybe yes. Maybe no. I think yes. What do you think?"

"What about building a family?"

"Yes, that comes first. Building our family." He smiles and tucks a strand of hair behind my ear.

I raise my eyebrows, but don't say anything.

"You are trying to tell me something, no?"

I nod and smile. "Yes, my love. If I'm not mistaken, our growing family will become larger next summer."

Brushing away tears, Agapito says, "Of course, I knew that this could happen. I am sorry, Dorcas. I can not help thinking of my darling, baby girl. My heart still aches for her." He twists his body and kisses me tenderly. "But my heart is finally ready to welcome a new baby girl."

"What if it is a boy?"

"I am sure that God will send us a little angel."

"Guess again, my love. I am told that we are to expect a mischievous little boy, one who is just like his daddy."

"Oh, so this is what you think of me? Now I know." He tickles me in a place that I had better not mention, and I tickle him back.

"Shush," I tell him. "We are not alone."

"This I know," he says. Then he says some words in Spanish that I don't recognize.

When he finishes and is quiet for a moment, I'm overcome with a feeling of good fortune. I have a wonderful family, lots of land, a future full of dreams and opportunities, a loving husband, and, Good heavens! Another baby on the way.

We've survived a horrible storm, but now I'm certain there's nothing that we can't accomplish together.

I rest my head on his shoulder and say, "The Christmas miracle I'm most grateful for is *you*, Agapito. My love. Goodnight."

He touches my cheek and smiles, "Merry Christmas, *mi amor*."

Thank you for reading *A Pioneer Christmas Beyond the Oregon Trail*. Here's hoping that you enjoyed spending Christmas with Dorcas and her family.

How about another rollicking adventure?

It's 1868. Grab your hat, step into your boots, and strap on those spurs. Your cow pony is saddled up and ready to ride the Chisholm Trail.

A brand-new cattle ranch drives its first herd to market. The trail is fraught with hazards from perilous river crossings to the mother of all stampedes. When the drovers realize that they're being tracked, followed, and hunted, a growing sense of doom overwhelms the fledgling outfit of wet-behind-the-ears cowboys.

Since they left San Antonio, the drovers have looked forward to whooping it up at the end of the trail. That was before somebody began killing cowboys. Now, Abilene seems like an impossible dream.

Will anybody make it to the end of the trail? Order *First Drive* today!

If you want to get your first look at this new adventure, claim your free copy of *Farewell to Poesta Creek*, a prequel novella.

Another Journey

Thanks for being a part of Dorcas, Agapito, Rose, Andrew, Christopher, and Dahlia Jane's first Christmas in Oregon.

Let's partner up for another exciting expedition. Get ready for a rollicking cattle drive adventure in 1868.

Order *First Drive* today. Snap the QR code and follow the trail to the author's website for more information.

GHOSTS ALONG THE OREGON TRAIL

If you haven't read the series, Ghosts Along the Oregon Trail, why not start today? Find out how it all began!

Delve into an unforgettable saga of empowerment, sacrifice, and the haunting echoes of a harrowing journey. Immerse yourself in an expedition where every decision carries the weight of life, death, and shattered dreams.

It all begins with *A Grave Every Mile*. Hop aboard!

About the Author

David Fitz-Gerald writes westerns and historical fiction. He is the author of more than a dozen books, including the series, Ghosts Along the Oregon Trail set in 1850. He's a multiple Laramie Award, first place, best in category winner; a Blue Ribbon Chanticleerian; a member of Western Writers of America; and a member of the Historical Novel Society.

Alpine landscapes and flashy horses always catch Dave's eye and turn his head. He is also an Adirondack 46-er, which means that he has hiked to the summit of the range's highest peaks. As a mountaineer, he's happiest at an elevation of over four thousand feet above sea level.

Dave is a lifelong fan of western fiction, landscapes, movies, and music. It should be no surprise that Dave delights in placing memorable characters on treacherous trails, mountain tops, and on the backs of wild horses.

Made in the USA
Monee, IL
18 December 2024

74531802R00073